D1243403

The Province of the Heart

# PHYLLIS McGINLEY

# The Province
of the Heart

PUBLISHED IN NEW YORK

THE VIKING PRESS

M    B    G

# Contents

## Contents

### FROM MY TERRACE

# The Province of the Heart

# The Other Side of the Shield:

## A NOTE TO THE READER

I CALL this introduction a Note rather than a Foreword or a Preface. For a Preface implies an apologia, an apologia implies an excuse, and I *have* no excuse for this book. All I can offer is an explanation of why, after twenty-five years of being a moderately respectable writer of verse, I should suddenly commit a collection of prose.

I'll be frank. It came about through my not knowing the right people in the literary world. If Mr. John Marquand, for instance, had been a close friend of mine, I could have called him on the telephone ten years ago when I finished reading one of his brilliant novels—I think it was *So Little Time*. Or I could have cornered him at a cocktail party and asked him face to face why he persisted in denigrating my suburb. For that is what he had been doing in his several satires which I so much admired—wittily naming and then demolishing in print the village where I lived and shopped for grapefruit and attended library meetings and weeded dandelions and composed my poems. I felt I knew that village better than he, and that it was not at all the dreary stronghold of mediocrity which he pictured, but a lively, interesting, and desirable dwelling-place. I felt it ought to be defended.

Since it seemed impossible to defend it in casual conversation, I took to my typewriter and wrote what was then considered a controversial article called "Suburbia, of Thee I Sing." *Harper's* magnanimously published it. It's amusing to recollect now, in a day when Suburbia has pretty well lost its stigma, when it overflows with novelists and actors and composers and even other poets as well as the stalwart citizens who have always recognized its merits, that what I said was then considered a formal heresy. That the heresy has become orthodoxy is certainly not due to my single-handed efforts. The tide was already running my way. But the reaction I got from a multitude of readers turned my head. (Their letters ranged from wild disagreement to assent so total that some writers asked me, please, to find them houses in that nice neighborhood. I thought for a while the local real-estate interests were about to elect me mayor.)

It was pleasant, being an Influence. I found out also what my friends had realized all along—that I was an opinionated woman. Those opinions, it was nice to know, I could air in hospitable magazines. From time to time I do so. I praised the younger generation or I deplored their bringing-up. I lauded a sense of sin. I inveighed against too early pairing-off among boys and girls and I enumerated the odd advantages of a bad education. On occasion I wrote with mild mockery as had been my custom in verse;

but most of the time I wrote out of a fairly passionate concern for tradition or morality. The result is this small book, in which I carry on a sort of running argument with those whose interpretation of life is different from mine.

I say "different." I do not say "untrue." There are many aspects to truth, and it is extremely difficult for anyone but God to observe them all at once. My version of a suburb, to take that first example, is probably not the whole picture. It is merely the one I look at from my own window and with the kind of eyes I have been given. I write about my own friends, acquaintances, experiences, family; about my neighbors and *their* neighbors. I investigate the province of one mind and one heart. My world is not the world of Graham Greene or the world of Tennessee Williams or even that of Mr. Marquand. But it is not an invention; it is my seen facet of reality.

I remember an old fable which used to appear often in schoolbooks of an earlier day. It concerns two knights who, riding from opposite directions, met at a crossroads or an inn or some sort of wayside shrine; the versions differ. At any rate, they found a shield there, suspended just above their heads on a standard, and the shield had on it a legend inscribed in Latin.

The two knights drew rein and saluted. Then each proceeded to decipher the writing aloud.

" 'Trust in God,' " read out the first. "A fine saying, friend."

"The saying may be good, but your Latin is vile, Sir

Knight," complained the second discourteously. "I'm no scholar, but I know 'Honor the King' when I see it. And that's what's on this shield."

The first knight was justly indignant. "Will you call me a liar, then?" he demanded fiercely. "You do so at your peril. I'm no pedant, either, but 'Trust in God' was the first slogan Merlin taught his pages. 'Honor the King,' indeed!"

"Then it's you are the liar," shouted the second even more fiercely. "A liar and an uneducated lout to boot. 'Honor' it says, and 'King' it says, and I'll see you dead in the dust before I'll deny it."

And with that the two brave fellows pulled down their visors, couched their lances, and fought until they were both stretched insensible in the roadway.

When spectators came to carry them off, it was discovered, of course, that both of them had been right and both wrong. The shield said exactly what each of them had contended: "Trust in God" on one side and "Honor the King" on the other.

I try to bear the parable in mind when enthusiasm for some cause threatens to carry me away. I cannot always see both sides of the shield from where I stand; but then, neither can my opponents. If my opinions are fallible, my arguments capable of being parried, so are those put forth by seers whose cast of mind is darker. These essays represent my personal reading of the truth.

Mine, I admit, is a cheerful truth. But then perhaps my intended role in life is to play the part of Mr. Edwards.

Mr. Edwards, you recall, was the "decent-looking elderly man in grey clothes" who once accosted Samuel Johnson in Butcher-row. The great man took the lesser one home with him, and they spent the afternoon in conversation. Surprisingly, it seems, to have been a real conversation rather than a monologue, for Boswell quotes Edwards' speeches at some length, including his famous retort.

"You are a philosopher, Dr. Johnson. I have tried too in my time to be a philosopher; but, I don't know how, cheerfulness was always breaking in."

# Unorthodoxies

# The Honor of Being a Woman

WHEN we had been married only a few months, my husband (moved by God knows what private and loving impulse) paid me the supreme compliment in his power.

"You know, dear," he remarked fondly, "you're a wonderful girl. You think like a man."

I can remember refuting him passionately. "But I don't! I *don't*. What a horrid thing to say!"

My outburst took us both by surprise. We laughed then and we laugh still when we recall it. But my denial, if overheated, was still the expression of a truth I had not until then really considered. I was, I am, a member of the nation of women. And in spite of our new freedoms, of all our recent skills and strengths and talents, we do not wish to belong to a different tribe. We do not want to think like men or feel like men or act like men—only like women and human beings.

Maintaining full citizenship in the feminine race, however, is becoming increasingly difficult. Suddenly enfranchised, hastily given the keys of all cities and all liberties, women resemble one of the new states created after a war. We have not owned our freedom long enough to know exactly how it should be used.

There is nothing original about my saying this. Women are currently the great topic of public conversation. We are being talked over until everyone is deafened by the noise of controversy. Scientists explain us. Anthropologists define our origins. Psychiatrists scold us. We are examined, analyzed, exhorted, bemoaned, and praised. Never, I think, since philosophers debated whether or not we had souls, have we been the subject of so much discussion.

If our heads swim occasionally, if we grow giddy with change, is it any wonder? We are urged to take our rightful place in the world of affairs. We are also commanded to stay at home and mind the hearth. We are lauded for our stamina and pitied for our lack of it. If we run to large families, we are told we are overpopulating the earth. If we are childless, we are damned for not fulfilling our functions. We are goaded into jobs and careers, then warned that our competition with men is unsettling both sexes.

I think sometimes with envy of the women of other eras who learned their duties and their limitations by prescription. They did not have electric dryers or the vote. They played tennis (if at all) in long skirts; and they would have fainted dead away at sight of a Bikini bathing suit. When they possessed fortunes, their husbands managed the money. But they knew what was expected of them. And they were aware what honor was due them.

It is in the matter of our honor that we have been

steady losers the last thirty or forty years. "Honor!" The very word has taken on a tinge of sentimentality. We have honors instead—prizes for writing novels or sailing boats or winning at golf or inventing advertising slogans or answering questions on television. We have our pictures in the papers for becoming Miss West Hohokus or Mrs. America. On one Sunday a year, with hysterical assistance from florists and candy-makers and greeting-card manufacturers, we are hailed as Mothers, a festivity about as comforting and comfortable as Walpurgis Night. Yet the ancient, almost mystical respect which was once paid us because we were the opposites of men has vanished along with base-burners and *Godey's Lady's Book.*

Have we done this thing to ourselves, or is it a natural outcome of the world's trends? When our grandmothers agitated for equal suffrage, when there were hunger strikes and jailings and long-skirted ladies marching with printed slogans in votes parades, was that the beginning of our uneasy status? Or would the times themselves have forced us to take up the terrible burden of equality which we now must carry? I do not know and I doubt even if the sociologists could tell us. But the burdens are clearly present, and all our shoulders sag a little. They sag because the equality is, actually, one in name only. Women, I contend, are not men's equals in anything except responsibility. We are not their inferiors, either, or even their superiors. We are quite simply different races. We live by an impulse separate from that of men. A separate tide beats in our blood. Our bodies are shaped to bear children, and our lives are a working-out of the processes of creation. All our ambitions and intelligence are beside that great elemental point. Yet, for the first time in history, society takes no cognizance of it.

Somewhere we have taken the wrong turning; somewhere along the path through this difficult world we have been misled. Chiefly the error is one of education.

Is a woman's training tailored for her needs and dispensations? Not at all. Her education is a hand-me-down from man's shelf, a garment unaltered and misfitting. From the moment a little girl skips off to school, she becomes a cog in an enormous system that was designed originally for boys. The system—the American one, at least—is a vast and noble experiment. It has been polestar and exemplar for other nations. But from kindergarten until she graduates from college the girl is treated in it exactly like her brothers. She studies the same subjects, becomes proficient at the same sports. Oh, it is a magnificent lore she learns, education for the mind beyond anything Jane Austen or Saint Theresa or even Mrs. Pankhurst ever dreamed. It is truly Utopian. But Utopia was never meant to exist on this disheveled planet.

The girl sees no difference between herself and the boys who surround her until, say, in the sixth grade, a kind of frightening flirtation begins at the very desk where she sits to copy down her long division.

Even in the private schools designed for girls alone, the only separation is physical. The subject matter is still identical with that of boys' schools. My own daughters, lately out of boarding school, might as well have gone to Exeter or Lawrenceville for all the difference in the curriculum between those academies and theirs. (Certainly manners were observed and speech supervised, but any masculine prep school stresses decorum also.) They learned Latin and mathematics and science and something called School Spirit and the kind of honor which means not tattling on their contemporaries. They learned how to take College Board examinations without trembling. They played hockey and basketball. They worked on magazines and edited year books, or they played Cyrano de Bergerac in the school play. Somewhere and at some time it became clear to them they were girls; but they learned that by ear, just as they acquired the ability politely to refuse an invitation over the phone or coax a boy away from the punch bowl at a holiday dance. So far as they knew, the privileges of life were theirs equally with those of their male comrades.

In college they suffer still the same delusions. Their liberties are scarcely more restricted than young men's; their courses are identical. This holds no less for women's colleges than for the great coeducational and state universities. In fact, I believe the students at women's colleges labor under an immenser illusion. At least the coed is aware that she is something of an appendage to men's activities. At Smith or Sarah Lawrence or Goucher, a girl herself is in charge of all affairs. The world she sees is a woman's world, and she is in competition with her own gender. No one except a superior woman can brush her aside or damage her expanding ego.

What happens, then, to these beautiful Amazons with their healthy bodies, their well-trained minds, their sense that the destiny of earth is in their hands?

The object in most cases is still matrimony. But if the girl in question does not immediately acquire a husband, or if she has an expendable talent or trade or a natural bent which she is eager to explore, she goes to the market place. There she is in for a shock. She discovers that this is still a masculine world, that most of the plums on the worldly tree are reserved for men only. Sixteen years out of her possible twenty-two have been given over to education, and this is her first lesson in the facts which most concern her! She may have headed her class in anthropology or business management or medicine. But she has to do more than say "Open, Sesame" at the doors of a profession. The gates which swing wide for young men contract narrowly for her.

"Take a secretarial course, my dear," advises the publisher to whom her literary aptitudes have sent her. "That's the only way to begin with our firm."

"Why not teach?" asks the vocational director when the mathematics major applies for a business job.

The medical student gets sent to the lesser schools. The young lawyer takes the position her male colleagues have declined. Oh! there are ways for a woman to succeed, and many do succeed. Women are alarmingly adaptable. But the price of success is often a grinding, gouging, knock-about struggle in which the essentially feminine quality is lost. And in the end it is only the truly gifted or the very dedicated who win through to the top. Even then they emerge wearing an extra shell—rather as if they were well-coated croutons popping up from the bottom of a furiously boiling kettle. I do not say it is a bad thing that the world should be so geared. It is functional and proper that ordinary prizes should be designed for men. I think merely that girls should be realistic as to their chances.

Not that it matters to most of them. For the majority of girls still marry, and marry young. With the ink scarcely dry on their diplomas, they hurl themselves into a vocation for which almost nothing has prepared them. Until now, I repeat, the pattern of our living has taught them to feel peers, partners, equals to men. Education has told them they owned no impediment as citizens or human beings—and granted them no extra honor. Wifehood is something they are expected to know by instinct. I do not refer to rudimentary skills. They have probably learned how to cook a bit or sew a rough seam. They have sat, for an outrageous fee, with neighborhood babies. But who has taught them that they are tools, not handlers; creatures subject to the caprices of fate and not mistresses of it? Have they learned what a woman chiefly needs—a terrible patience, a vast tolerance, forgivingness, forbearance, an almost divine willingness to forget private wants in the needs of her family? The lucky ones are born with that knowledge. The less atavistic have to study in the hardest of schools. Some never get it. Then follow the recriminations and self-pity, the divorce court or the analyst's couch. No one who looks at the divorce rate in our country can feel complacent over American marriage or American education, either.

For, say what you will, making marriage work is a woman's business. The institution was invented to do her homage; it was contrived for her protection. Unless she accepts it as such—as a beautiful, bountiful, but quite unequal association—the going will be hard indeed.

How can it be otherwise when modern society conspires to *make* it difficult? Boys and girls marry before they are financially stable, upsetting the ancient tradition that a man must have a house of his own to which he brings his bride. The young wife, in turn, trained to make not a home but a living, becomes his working comrade. She either shoulders the double burden of wage-earning and house-keeping, or she presses him into being half-housewife. The whole machinery of marriage is upset. Or else the children come and domesticity closes in about her like a Bastille. Servants are few and expensive, nor can gadgets replace them. And since she has not been taught the honor of her station, her disabilities rasp upon her and disfigure happiness.

"It isn't fair!" is the commonest cry of the newly married young. It isn't fair that arts and erudition should come to nothing, stifled by the necessities of ordinary household tasks. Well, of course it's not fair from their angled viewpoint. They should have been told long ago that life is seldom fair, and that woman's chief honor is to know that and be able to surmount it. What foolish mentor has taught a girl to believe that life either owed her anything or was willing to hand it to her upon a salver? "Share your husband's interests," she *has* been instructed. So she can beat him at golf or listen knowledgeably to a Mozart opera or make a good partner at bridge. But is she equal to meeting him at the door after a day of frustrations—of demon antic among the young, of cakes and formulas spoiled and cleaning women who did not appear—and listen honorably to the story of *his* trials and disappointments? Can she watch him discipline the children and not obviously interfere? Can she treat him, in other words, like a husband and not a clumsy intruder or the person responsible for her woes? If she has once worked in an office, she knows that business holds no rougher ordeals than does a housekeeping existence. She understands what one saint—I believe it was an Ursuline nun—was getting at in a sentence I recall only well enough to paraphrase. This saint had entered the monastic life after having first been married, widowed, and forced to earn a living for her young son.

"Nothing," she exclaimed candidly, "in the rigors of a convent community can equal, for difficulty, the day-by-day exasperations of household living."

Three centuries have not changed the truth of her observation. Rather, they have underlined it; for now the exasperations come as a surprise. The girl today had expected matrimony to be something like an incorporated business and she herself nothing less than the chairman of the board. Instead she is office girl, clerk, drudge, as well as underpaid and overworked executive. The term "part-ner" is a fallacy.

For, as I have said elsewhere, women err when they regard marriage as an equal partnership. That error becomes compounded when it extends—as it has done increasingly—into the most secret places of her womanhood, into the sanctuaries of sex.

I do not know who first invented the myth of sexual equality. But it is a myth willfully fostered and nourished by certain semi-scientists and other fiction writers. And it has done more, I suspect, to unsettle marital happiness than any other false doctrine of this myth-ridden age. In a perfect marriage, one supposes, body and mind unite from the beginning in absolute communion with no stumbling blocks to pleasure or to comprehension. Alas, there are few perfect things on earth. A young wife can be deeply, truly in love with her husband and yet find that her responses are slower than his, less natively ardent. She is, in fact, a wholly normal woman. Her abilities are not his. But the pair of them have listened all their lives to the New Mythology. It has been thundered at them by self-appointed marriage counselors and the seedier psychiatrists. It has been screeched at them by sensational novelists and tract-writers: a less than fiery woman is a frigid one.

Frigidity is largely nonsense. It is this generation's catchword, one only vaguely understood and constantly misused. Frigid women are few. There is a host of diffident and slow-ripening ones. The very planet would have tipped out of orbit long ago (from sheer overpopulation) if there were no innate differences in strength and continuity of desire between the sexes. But so heavy is the hold of a half-truth that the girl brought up in her equal world to believe herself no different from a man in capability is shamed, frightened, and bewildered by what she thinks is her own lack. Her husband is disappointed or resentful. So many a marriage which in a less gullible era would have turned out happily, totters and falls apart over a perfectly natural disparity.

The consummation of love in the flesh is a great, a compelling and magnificent act. But it has been sentimentalized out of all proportion. It is not the whole of love nor is it the whole of marriage. To believe otherwise is to degrade man, woman, and society. That I am speaking a kind of modern heresy I am aware. But this heresy has been orthodoxy in other eras and will be so again. It is good that prudery has vanished. It will be better when the exaggeration of sex as such subsides into realism—when girls who long ago ceased behaving like heroines out of a Victorian novel also leave off imitating one of O'Hara's or Hemingway's lady rakes.

The philosopher Jacques Maritain, in his *Reflections on America*, sets forth some of our national illusions. High on his list is the illusion "that marriage must be both the perfect fulfillment of romantic love and the pursuit of full individual self-realization for the two partners involved."

And right he is, at least as regards women. Men may be allowed romanticism; women, who can create life in their own bodies, dare not indulge in it. Nor can they safely seek self-realization at all costs. If they do, the family suffers first, and then the nation, and ultimately the world.

How do we reverse the trends, then? How do we alter education so that it will emphasize differences as well as likenesses between the genders? I do not know, but somehow it must be managed. Women have been enfranchised now for nearly forty years. But the world is no better for our free participation in it. Marriages made for love seem no more durable than those once arbitrarily arranged. Violence and crime and cruelty exist as they always have. And if we have brought no new graces to our society, if we are losing the old ones, we have no right to our rights.

Perhaps we shall have to start earning them all over again. Our greatest victories have always been moral ones. Without relinquishing our new learning or our immediate opportunities, we must return to a more native sphere. Let us teach our daughters not self-realization at any cost but the true glory of being a woman—sacrifice, containment, pride, and pleasure in our natural accomplishments. Let us win back honor. The honors will take care of themselves.

# Babes in Arms

W H E N I was eleven years old, my clothes weren't much of a problem. At school, in pleated skirt and middy blouse, I was indistinguishable from my friends; and for Sundays there was always that nice blue serge. I recollect an occasional burst of high fashion for holidays and birthday parties—usually black velveteen with a lace collar. But what to put on in the evening was no concern at all. I didn't go out in the evening. Not until fifteen, when I cut a less than dazzling swath at the junior prom, did I attain the unimaginable glory of a genuine evening dress.

That was a long time ago, of course, in what my daughters used to refer to as "the olden days." But something more than a generation in time divides my notion of a girl's wardrobe from theirs.

At eleven they were already agonizing over what they should wear to the Friday-night dancing class. Whatever turned out to be their choice, it had to be "formal," and it demanded a pair of silver slippers and some sort of special wrap for accompaniment. At fifteen, even my younger had outgrown a whole closetful of tulle and taffeta numbers with slippers dyed to match. And all this in a middle-class household, in a middle-class community, without aspirations toward anything except normal suburban folkways.

Who is dour enough to doubt that little girls look delightful dressed so? Who will deny that the most enchanting sight in the world is a twelve- or thirteen-year-old swirling off to a Christmas ball enveloped in a pastel cloud, a touch of lipstick on her curving mouth, her thin little arms bare, a corsage pinned tightly to her flat little bosom? Well, I, for one, deny it. I admit it's pretty, and I think it's perfectly absurd.

You may ask, then, Why do I put up with it? You may ask, that is. But if you really *need* to inquire you are either no mother or a more formidable one than any I have encountered. I have grudgingly permitted it—I have even shopped for the wardrobe—because this sort of premature social life is the pattern in our village and, I am beginning to believe, on our continent.

The clothes are the symbol. Something unwholesome has crept into the American cult of adolescence. If childhood is still a state, it is now chiefly a state of confusion. On the surface everything looks well. Never before has the youngest generation seemed so healthy, so handsome and intelligent. Pink-cheeked and shiny-haired, bursting with vitamins and social consciousness, they march toward the future like a race of under-age Utopians. But the confusion is apparent and springs from a real cause. For not only have our children been exposed to every wind that blows from the bleak heights of Educational Theory; not only does the Gospel according to Saint Psychology change from season to season and from apostle to apostle; children are also expected to stay children longer, and at the same time to become adults sooner, than ever before in history.

I leave to philosophers and anthropologists the task of explaining the larger riddle of why, in an era when people expect to live longer and longer, when the age of financial responsibility comes later and later, our young keep marrying earlier and earlier. It probably has something to do with the atom bomb or sunspots and has no proper part in these pages. What does concern me is how we keep lowering the age of courtship.

Admitted, it's perfectly normal at a certain period—say in the fifth or sixth grade—for boys and girls to discover there are two genders. They discover it with amazement and bewildered joy, like Balboa encountering the Pacific or a baby observing his first snowfall. In my time this was the interlude of having one's books fetched home from school and being teased at recess. I remember one Lothario who, to my intense embarrassment, kept helping me off with my galoshes and lending me his bicycle. After a season of such sheepish gestures as huge tributes in the school valentine box, the fever spent itself. He and I went back to playing baseball on the same Saturday team and gradually forgot our flaming affair.

Not so this generation. Abetted, indeed pushed and prodded and egged on by their mothers or the P.T.A. or scoutmasters, sixth-grade children are now making dates on the telephone and ineptly jitterbugging together every week-end evening. I think it's called "adjusting." But to me and to a few other parents there is something grotesque about the whole business. These are children parodying the behavior of grownups. What's more, they follow the pattern not willingly in most cases, but out of obedient conformity—and sometimes against their wills.

They are taking on a burden before they are capable of bearing it. Just how unsettling it can be was brought home to me some seasons ago when one of my two daughters was turning eleven. Somehow the local Boy Scouts had become infected with the social virus. Someone had decided that a dance instead of a powwow would be a good thing. So each Scout (most likely under penalty of being stripped of his medals in full view of the troop) had been directed to bring a girl.

Now this particular daughter is full of curly charms—curly hair, curling eyelashes, a tongue curly with tact. So three Scouts, each equally clean, courteous, friendly, loyal, reverent, and squeaky-voiced, demanded the privilege of escorting her. A handful of years later she would have savored the moment. It reduced her, then, to tears. The dilemma, not only of what to wear, what to say, but of how to refuse two of them politely, overcame her.

Out of patience as I was with the whole idea, I still took time to advise her. And I ended by explaining just what I thought of the local Ward McAllister who had dreamed up the affair.

"You're too young to have to deal with these things seriously," I said. "It's too much responsibility for you."

She collapsed, sobbing, on the day bed.

"I know. I know," she cried. "I just want to have my childhood!"

And, allowing for a certain amount of dramatic exaggeration, she was telling the truth.

She wanted, as I believe most young adolescents want, another year or two of the free, uncompetitive give-and-take of life.

Except for the precocious few, children *do* value childhood. Left to himself, the average boy would, after that first fine, careless rapture of the fifth grade, far prefer to spend his afternoons with a baseball mitt and his evenings poring over plans for a model airplane than listening to rock-'n-roll records at a mixed party. And the average girl, left to *herself*, would choose feminine chitchat to flirtation. But they are *not* left to themselves. They are coaxed and bullied and enticed into "mingling." There are school dances and church dances and Scout dances. There are Coke parties and local "assemblies" and what passes for dances at private homes. By the time they enter junior high school they are devastatingly conscious of social achievement. At high-school age, they have become either blasé veterans or shamefaced failures.

The quiet boys have become quieter—turned, maybe, into sulky little misogynists—while the Lotharios swagger worse than ever. Early-ripened Juliets preen like peacocks and hold court, while their shier sisters wear defeat as if it were a dunce's cap and loathe their A-cup brassières. They are allowed no time to mold themselves gradually or to grow shells for self-protection. The fact that at eighteen the undersized boy will probably be a long-limbed giant, or that at seventeen the tongue-tied girl once obscured by freckles and braces on her teeth will be turning the heads of college men, does not compensate for early scars.

Whatever happened, anyhow, to the notion that being "boy-struck" (or more occasionally, "girl-struck") was a deplorable, even if not unnatural, phase of adolescence? There always used to be one buxom girl, ringleted and knowing, whom parents viewed with alarm. The one I recall was named Rosemary. She constituted the neighborhood bad example. It was Rosemary who rang boys up on the telephone and lingered late with them on snowy slopes in winter and always suggested the kissing games at birthday parties. The Rosemary I knew married a brakeman before she was eighteen and is now a cheerful grandmother. But I see her incarnation constantly, for she has become the Ideal Girl.

It's the miss who *isn't* boy-struck over whom mothers wring their hands.

"I don't know what I'm to do about Lucy," a friend of mine clucked to me recently. "She simply won't invite anybody to the Youth Center Barn Dance. And she won't even listen to me when I try to plan a party for her and invite some boys."

Lucy at twelve is currently small and speechless. She'll be a charmer one day if she is permitted to continue her romance with tropical fish for a while longer. She hasn't at present the faintest interest in anything male unless it lives in an aquarium. If she could, of course, meet Gilbert, another fish-fancier, she might well give him her soul's devotion. But Gilbert is also being chivied by *his* mother. She wishes like anything that he'd go willingly to the weekly soirées her friends' daughters are contriving. He needs, she asserts, more "wholesome contacts." And nothing can persuade her that Gilbert's point of view is a good deal more wholesome than hers.

For there is even an uglier aspect to this picture than the surface one. The fumbling acts of courtship have a new name in every generation. Our grandmothers spoke of "spooning." My generation discussed "necking." Today I believe it's referred to as "making out" and seems to be as commonplace a feature of grade-school and junior-high-school parties as the shoeless dancers and the Coke bottles. Actually I find this less shocking than ridiculous. I cannot think that even the most advanced subteen couples kissing in a darkened library are doing more than aping something they have seen on television or in a comic book. But the darkened rooms are part of the picture. So is a lack of chaperonage. By the time a girl has turned thirteen, she is, if she has the makings of a belle, already adept at turning aside the clumsy pawings of little boys. (Or perhaps she has learned how to encourage them.) In my own household, when I found out what an invitation to a mixed party entailed, I solved the problem partially by a few phone calls. No chaperon, no acceptance. But the miasma of amorous gossip hangs over adolescence like smog.

I suppose I should have been happy about her social competence when one daughter confided to me, at thirteen, how she managed at parties to steer clear of wolves, junior grade, without loss of prestige.

"I just bring along some extra records and get the boys to go out in the hall with me and do the Lindy."

Instead I grieved over innocence so soon tarnished.

It is difficult to know exactly whom to blame for the grotesque situation. The parents? The community? The climate of the times? But ours is the most respectable of communities, and these are devoted parents. Moreover, the age is not really profligate. Probably we are all the culprits. (Only the children we cannot blame, for they are our creations.) Books, radio, television, magazines, and movies have had their impact. But chiefly, I think, the situation results from our overemphasis on the very rights of childhood, which we are so oddly abusing. This age must be the happy time, we are warned. It must be the time for "integration into the group." Boys and girls must learn to be playmates and friends; there must be no social misfits, no deviations from an imaginary norm. We make no allowances for time lags and individual preferences. Infants at three months need bananas in their daily diet. So at exactly eleven and a half (or whatever the book says) girls should begin to take an interest in boys, and vice versa.

Or perhaps there is a meaner reason. Perhaps the mothers' competitive instincts are doing the driving. Too many parents, maybe, are holding fast to youth by vicariously reliving it through their children. Popularity and belledom are the golden goals; and the young are being trained for it as athletes are trained for the Olympics. This concept of early failure or success can damage wickedly. At eleven or twelve or thirteen, what child is capable of making a social judgment? The judgment, though, is forced upon them. So the shy or awkward boy may become convinced of his eternal ineptitude before his voice has changed, and the girl learn to be a wallflower before her petals have begun to open.

The answer to the problem? I have no easy one except to let the schools or the parents meddle less and chaperon more. Or if early marriage is the prize, let these embryo candidates be thrust less upon one another. This greenhouse forcing is neither natural nor wise. Let social age and not textbook age determine the time for bringing the genders together. It might be well to fetch back the duenna and let the mixed party be a special and guarded treat. I warrant we shall all be more comfortable, parents and children alike. For, plan as we wish, set the sexes dancing together as often and as early as we can, they will mingle without self-consciousness only after adolescence has passed or before it has yet begun. Perhaps *only* at the earlier time. For uninhibited valor in the chase one must look to the second-grade set. My other daughter once astonished us at dinner (when she was seven) with the announcement that Billy Brown had kissed her after class.

"He did?" we asked in a raised-eyebrows sort of voice.

"Yes, he did," said the unblushing maiden. "Three girls helped me catch him."

With the huntress in woman so well demonstrated, I think we need not fear that many of our girls will turn out spinsters. All girls—with a little assistance from orthodontists, dermatologists, and dietitians—are now beautiful. And all the brothers are valiant. It seems to me we might do better to teach them how also to be intelligent and modest and kind than to train them solely for the social arena. A girl will make a fitter wife, perhaps, if the tulle-and-silver-slippers phase comes a bit later in her life than the sixth grade. And a boy may value manhood more when he does not get his first dinner jacket at thirteen. Who knows? It could be that a majority of them, like my daughter, might just want to have their childhood.

# In Defense of Sin

MOTHERS, even the wisest of them, are improvident creatures; they never really believe their children will grow up. It isn't that they do not plan. Their lives are feverish with planning, the paths behind them littered with discarded maps and charts and abandoned strategies. It is simply that parenthood is such a hand-to-mouth existence, such a series of skirmishes won (or lost), that they can only live, like soldiers in the field, from day to day.

Sufficient unto the hour is the crisis thereof. Babies must cut molars, kindergartners start off to school, little boys break windows, and little girls their hearts at dancing class. Each peril has to be faced as it is encountered—the first fib, the measles, the naughty word, the sprained ankle, and the explanation of sex. Puppies get run over, teachers are unjust, cronies turn out to be faithless; and every event is an emergency for which there can be no real preparation except love and common sense.

And then suddenly a mother looks about her and her children are children no longer. This is a curious moment, compounded in almost equal portions of exhilaration, panic, and surprise. In the ascent of her particular Everest, she has reached a sort of plateau, and there is triumph in that. But as she peers back at the trail by which she has come—at all the little peaks surmounted and chasms crossed—what a safe and pleasant climb it appears in retrospect!

Even the most desperate situation had this consolation —that however inadequate her hand, it was there to be reached for. She could interpose herself between the child and life.

Now that must change. Our daughters (for since I have only daughters, I must speak of the gender I know best) must climb the rest of the way very nearly unaccompanied, and it wrings the heart. Perhaps they have not quite recovered from adolescence. They are still unsure of themselves. They still keep diaries, which they lock away in secret drawers. They worry about their complexions and are touchy about their friends and take a gentle suggestion as a personal affront. But they have driving licenses and a clothes allowance; and the boys they bring home are growing up to their ears and speak condescendingly to adults in manly voices. Next year or the year after will bring college or a job. It will also bring either love or its facsimile.

What then shall I, what shall any mother, give them for an amulet against the dangerous journey they must take alone? For we know, unfashionable as it may be to say so, that the dangers are real. Thousands of textbooks; editorials in the press; papers read to learned societies; a whole new profession of consultants on the matter, often attached to the schools—all these, plus the conversation of the young themselves, attest their genuineness.

Surely no one would be naïve enough to think that little biological chats about conception and bodily structure are sufficient. Our daughters have known for a long time just how babies are born, and have accepted, we hope, their theoretical knowledge of sex gravely and sweetly. But the tides of spring run strong. Home ties are breaking off, and to the confusion of new voices and circumstances and the competition for popularity will be added the pulse of their own blood. Curiosity, even, will have its urgent pull.

Admitted that illicit sexual adventure is a peril, at least for what used to be called "marriageable girls," what memorable word can we teach them that they can repeat like an incantation if the tide should become a threatening flood?

I have talked this over with friends and psychologists. I have read the brochures and the textbooks. I have also thought about the problem deeply, and I know what I, for one, shall do. It's a very iconoclastic thing; it has not been mentioned at all in any of the dozens of pamphlets and tomes I have dipped into. But it seems sanest. I shall remind my daughters simply that there is such a thing as right and such a thing as wrong. I shall commit the dreadful heresy of talking about sin.

Sin has always been an ugly word, but it has been made so in a new sense over the last half-century. It has been made not only ugly but passé. People are no longer sinful, they are only immature or underprivileged or frightened or, more particularly, sick. And I think it has no doubt been helpful to some unfortunates to find themselves so considered. But my daughters and yours are fairly brave and certainly privileged and more mature than we might have hoped; and if their souls had been sick, we should have known it before this. *My* children would believe themselves mortally insulted to have their misdemeanors classified as illnesses. In our household we have never been afraid of sin as a common noun.

In fact, although until now we have never used the word in connection with matters of sex, we have found it a subject of fruitful discussion. We think it is sinful to slander our neighbors. We believe that stealing and cheating and bearing false witness are sins. We think dishonest politicians are sinners. Once, when intolerance raised its unattractive head, we disposed of it readily. We refused to repeat all the windy arguments that have become the standard clichés; we just said that anti-Semitism, like every other artificial bias against one's fellow man, is a sin. And that—as nearly as is humanly possible—was that.

Oddly enough I find little opposition to this last stand among the schoolbook coterie. If they decline to mention sin in connection with prejudice, they do consent to speak of "erroneous social thinking." But not once, in any text, did I come across a reference to either right or wrong in regard to the great act of love. Most of the books naturally deplore sexual experiment. They use all the commonplace arguments. They point out the physical dangers, the emotional involvement, the inconveniences and distresses of furtive passion.

And while some writers I find inane to the point of vulgarity (one author even suggested coy things to say to "break off a petting session"), others have set down superbly reasoned appeals for chastity. But how strong is reason against a tidal wave? I think conscience proves a superior shelter. My daughters shall be told that there exist a moral law and an ancient commandment and that they do wrong to flout them.

And now against my critics (who will be many if they are well versed in the gospel that had its ultimate evangelist in Dr. Kinsey) I should like to argue the wholesomeness of treating extramarital relations as sinful. For that is what I do consider such teaching—wholesome and even effective.

To begin with, sin implies goodness, and the young love goodness with all their hearts. We all know what idealists they are, how fiercely they react against injustice and cruelty, how they hate hypocrisy and cant. To take away their delight in virtue, to tell them that they must withstand temptations because temptations are merely urges toward immature behavior, is to give them stones when they pant for bread. It is to weaken the muscles of their characters.

In the second place, it is confusing. I think we have all argued too much with our children in this generation. It has been drummed into our ears that we must explain the reasons behind every taboo, and we in turn have drummed these reasons into their ears until they are nearly deafened. I remember my older daughter, when she was small, once listening quietly to my careful dissertation on why some action was not to be tolerated. Finally she burst out, "Oh, Mother, why don't you just tell me not to for once and stop explaining!" Just so. It is simpler to treat sex morally than reasonably. Moreover, believing in sin is a kind of tactful armor. A girl might find, in a given situation, that it was better to tell a young man that he was doing wrong than that he was being a social dunce. His self-esteem would suffer less.

"But how about guilt?" ask my opponents. "When the young believe in sin, they must necessarily feel guilty if they commit it. Is not that destructive?"

From my fallible viewpoint, I do not think so. For sin implies forgiveness. One who has done a wrong can be sorry and recover. If he is generous enough, he can even forgive himself. But how does one go about forgiving oneself for a lapse in taste or a gaucherie? We have all committed sins in our lives, meannesses and angers and lies. But most of us have forgotten them easily. What we find hard to forget or to forgive are the silly things we have said, the times we have been awkward and doltish. It is one of my articles of psychological faith that a girl (and perhaps the same thing applies to a boy) would find life less broken apart after a misguided love affair if she could feel that she had been sinful rather than a fool. And I hope that all our daughters are sure enough of parental love not to let a sense of guilt destroy them in silence.

Now all this does not mean that because I am, like Coolidge's minister, against sin, I am also against sex or that my girls will get that impression. On the contrary, they will believe, I hope, that it is one of the moving graces of the world, far too magnificent a gift to be carelessly handled. We three women in our house are proud of being women. We feel a little sorry for men, who can never bear children or be wives. So when I mention the moral standard, they will understand that it is for the sake of protecting this magnificence that mankind has slowly, strugglingly, been building for several thousand years. Fashions in morals fluctuate. Puritan rigor gives way to Restoration license, and that in turn is drowned in Victorian severity. It is possible that much of our own permissive nonsense will be frowned on by the generation now growing up. But right and wrong do not really alter, nor do their consequences. And of this my daughters must be aware.

So what in the end shall I tell my daughters about chastity before marriage? Of *course*, I shall be sensible and point out the ordinary social penalties attached to any other conduct. I shall touch on the possible pregnancy, the untidiness, and the heartbreak. But I shall also say that love is never merely a biological act but one of the few miracles left on earth, and that to use it cheaply is a sin.

In fact that is what I have already told them.

# The Brave Generation

WE HAVE recently acquired a new member of our household. Her name is Bridie Walsh, she is eighteen or just a little over, and she comes to us straight from Galway on the rocky west coast of Ireland. Bridie is a pretty, pink-cheeked girl with a gentle voice and charming manners. For a woman's wages she does a woman's work; and besides being an efficient engineer of dishwashers and vacuum sweepers, she gives promise of becoming a really talented cook. She is also the pleasantest of companions.

Until Bridie was six years old she knew no English— only the soft Gaelic which we constantly coax her to speak for us. Urban regions are new to her. So are all the (to us) familiar gadgets in which she takes such naïve delight— the electric mixer, the ice-crusher, the toaster which is also a small oven. Even the public library and the television set are surprising treats. Bridie has lived in this country exactly four months. Yet already she is thoroughly at home with us and in America. She dresses smartly, can explore the city on Thursdays, has established friends and amusements and a bank account. We are all delighted to have her in the family but are a bit overawed by her self-possession. Could our daughters, we wonder, could their friends, could any young American of Bridie's age (and given the same compulsions) prove at once so intrepid and so adjustable? Could they accommodate themselves with such speed and generosity to a totally new environment?

The answer, I feel sure, is "Yes," an emphatic "Yes." This is a notable generation coming of age in our time. I have watched them growing up; I have listened to their conversation and marked down their exploits. And they have my unstinted admiration. Somewhat to my astonishment, I believe they could accomplish anything they put their capable hands to.

I say astonishment advisedly. All the signs pointed to a different outcome for the children of our day. Overindulged, wildly experimented upon, socially stimulated beyond their bent, they should by rights have turned into hedonists or barbarians. They have never known what it was to live upon a peaceful earth. Theirs has always been one of cold wars or hot conflict, an era of the most savage change since Rome began to totter on its foundations. Yet observe them now, the large majority of them—healthy, altruistic, energetic, virtuous, controlled, and on fire to help a world which they certainly had little share in making and one which at any moment may blow up in their faces.

"Show us these paragons," shout the criers of doom. "Who are they? *Where* are they, and what are they doing at this moment?"

The response is easy. They are all around us, in every conceivable situation. They are not, of course, the delinquents or the confused or psychotic young people who make headlines. From empty vessels proceeds the loudest noise, and those we read about in newspapers or hear debated on television are the sad exceptions. I do not refer to them but to my children and yours.

They are the boys on morning buses with books under their arms and suddenly deep voices. They are the girls in charm bracelets and pony-tails on their way to class. They are young wives working in offices to support their student husbands; and young men in beards, discussing the state of the universe. They are mowers of lawns, sitters with neighborhood babies, the apprentices at summer theaters and the guarders of summer beaches. They are waitresses at resort hotels, dissectors in laboratories, applicants for seminaries or service stations. Last spring they were crowding forty at a time into telephone booths for a mass caper. This fall they are crowding equally enthusiastically into teeming universities. They build hi-fi sets, dance to rock-'n-roll, write novels, pore over Proust or science fiction. They ride Vespas, drive tiny foreign cars; or they walk trails with packs on their backs. They are the girls chalking up their hundred hours of volunteer work in clinics and boys tutoring their way across the Atlantic Ocean. They are the pluckers of classic guitars, the admirers of Mozart or cool jazz, the devotees of Melville or Salinger. They are ordinary teen-agers, their minds on the evening's movie. And they are interns in fashionable hospitals, planning to be medical missionaries to Africa. They are scholars and playboys and careerists and evangelists, combaters of segregation, apostles against reaction and civic corruption.

They are immoderately learned for their age. Their talk is full of references to the rise of Stuart drama, the existentialism of Paul Tillich, the music of Béla Bartók. They are mad for dangerous sport—skating, sky-diving, spelunking. They are the takers of difficult examinations, the winners of fellowships; or they are blithe members of the armed services. They work too hard, study too much, pick too many flaws in the social system. They also pair off too young, marry too soon, have too many children too early. But by and large they are wonderful.

They are the brave generation, the children for whom we scarcely deserve to take credit. Compared to the tribal customs of my own youth, their ways are civilized beyond anything I recall.

At seventeen, for instance (which is as early as one can begin to perceive the shape of a human being), my companions and I were as limp and selfish a congregation as ever danced a fox-trot or talked back to our elders. We were, I expect, fairly harmless. But we were the worst of drifters. We spent our school years doing as little classwork as possible and our summers driving about aimlessly in somebody's car in the company of as many boys or girls as we could manage to get together. Popularity was all. If we traveled we went docilely with our families. Nobody took a job who did not need one. We were planning on college, most of us, but not for intellectual purposes. Our heads were full of dreams about fraternity parties and campus escapades and the possibilities of acquiring a diploma without—as the jargon had it then—ever "cracking a book." Genuine students were referred to slightingly as "deep thinkers," and we avoided them. It occurred to none of us to give our free time to helping in an orphanage or a hospital, or to see the world by our own wits. Seventeen was the resting-place between childhood and marriage, in a safe, undemanding world.

But, "Seventeen!" I overheard a young siren of my acquaintance exclaim on her birthday a year ago. "I'm seventeen! And what have I done with my life?"

Her remark was heartfelt. She and her generation understand the shortness of life, feel an urgency of accomplishment as few children have ever done before. Parties, romantic meetings, amusements are all very well. Being human, the young know their value. But they want much, much more. They long to see their talents exercised, their abilities extended, their virtues put to use. This girl had spent a rigorous school year, and I, coming from a different era, felt she deserved a summer's lazy holiday. She vetoed the idea. Instead, she invented and successfully manipulated a secretarial job for herself which kept her solvent and busy for most of the season. In her spare time she took part in community theatricals, studied ceramics, learned to play the piano, and was kind to her young men. She is not unusual. They all work these days; for wages if they can get them, for charity if they can't.

It is not that they are Puritans, valuing work for its own sake in the old Calvinistic sense. They value leisure too, so long as leisure does not mean lethargy. "The world is small and growing smaller," they seem eternally to be telling themselves. "But it is full of beauty and peril and excitement and we mustn't miss a bit of it." So when they are not going to school or drawing part-time salaries (or even while they are) they contrive to travel, for one thing. They see the world on ridiculously small amounts of money, put up cheerfully with improbable hardships. They act as nursemaids, as companions; they play in orchestras on liners. They tramp, bicycle, hitchhike. They spend their nights in youth hostels or sleeping bags, their days learning a new language or a foreign custom. Boys and girls alike, they are hardy as Marines and equally apt to have a current situation well in hand.

Last vacation half the young people I knew were abroad, traveling on their own earnings, on fellowships, scholarships, or as members of a field service or the Putney Experiment in International Living. Many of their elders may have been on the same continent with them too— hung with cameras and complaining about hotel reservations or the lack of ice and orange juice. The young were not complaining at all. They were climbing Welsh mountains, trudging in English rain, making friends in India or Sweden, helping with the work in a French farmhouse. What was exceptional or adventurous in my day is now the norm.

The dwindling of distances and the accessibility of other

countries may account for this generation's urge to explore. It does not account for their drive toward the intellectual life.

Nothing about them is so rewarding as this phenomenon. They are thirsty for learning, greedy for education. Schools, colleges cannot keep up with their demands. It is they rather than parents or teachers or heads of foundations who are begging for richer curricula and a severer course of study. I listen to high-school students complaining that they were not taught a foreign language in the lower grades or that the sciences for which they are now enrolled are not sufficiently comprehensive. I hear young men and women in colleges inveighing against a system which limits them to four or five subjects a term. "We could go faster. We could learn so much more if we were permitted," they insist.

In my day it would have been social death to admit to intellectual pretensions. One did one's studying by stealth, earned a genteel C, and wrote for the college magazine under a pseudonym. To audit a course for pleasure was unheard of. Our heroes, our heroines were the football stars and the Queens of the Homecoming Games. Now the more popular or recondite college courses overflow with auditors on the prowl for another crumb of information— a different interpretation of Joyce, further illumination on Kierkegaard, some famous professor's theory of astrophysics. Career athletics bear a certain stigma, and the situation has grown so serious that at some universities coaches must beat the bushes and issue plaintive communiqués in order to assemble any team at all. And while athletics wilt, the gentler arts flourish like a whole forest of green bay trees. The drama, symphonic music, painting, ballet—groups for the promulgation of those spring up on every campus as mushrooms sprout after rain. Freshmen write plays, blond coeds admit to composing poetry, everybody at least pretends to an affection for Bach or Richard Dyer-Bennet, Marc Chagall or El Greco, the Symbolists or the Cavaliers. Some of these affections, as I imply, may well *be* pretense. But they show the direction of the wind.

Nor are energy and intellectualism the only qualities of this admirable age. I own no statistics concerning their sexual behavior. The young are probably no better and no worse than their predecessors. They talk a good deal about sex. They read about it *ad nauseam* in novels written by their elders. But because they marry younger than they used to, I should venture a guess that promiscuity, at least, is on the wane. Moreover, religion is rapidly becoming respectable. There is a slackening-off of the scorn which was for a while accorded orthodox belief. So discipline may be tempering their actions as it did not for many years. And in any case I think their actual morality is decidedly higher than was ours.

For we must always remember that morality is not confined to one famous single Commandment. There happen to be ten precepts in the Decalogue, and three of them, particularly, rank high in the regard of this generation. There's the commandment about brotherly love and the one about honesty and the one about not bearing false witness against our neighbors. Concerning these they are fanatics.

If segregation, for instance, is on its deathbed, it's the young who are administering the *coup de grâce*. Senates may legislate, reformers proselyte, but it's boys and girls who keep making the vision a faint reality. To them the thought of discriminating against a contemporary because of his color or his religion is an offense that cries to their ardent heaven. Their parents may close the schools in the South. The young petition to open them. When a fraternity chapter loses its charter because it has elected a Negro or a Jew or possibly a Catholic, it's the alumni who have done the closing, not the undergraduates. Daily, in dormitories, factories, offices, classrooms, youth is living out the one great lesson it has truly learned—that all men are brothers.

And they are ruthlessly honest. *Because* they are young, they sometimes confuse tact with hypocrisy, politeness with dissimulation. They have not practiced compromise. So they are shocked to find their parents being civil to bores or flattering a useful acquaintance. They think doing a bit of mild jugglery with an income-tax form an outright felony. They despise people who fib about their ages, and they consider gossip degrading.

They also consider materialism the worst of sins. One hears a good deal these days about this generation's lack of commercial drive, the frame of mind popularly described as "beat." Businessmen deplore it and complain that young

job-applicants incline to look for security rather than for
risks and rewards; that they shrug their shoulders at conformity and Horatio Alger eagerness and the belief that
one should die for the dear old firm. But it isn't that the
generation is unambitious. Their ambitions lie in a direction opposed to ours. Theirs is a simplified, a secular version of the old query, "What shall it profit a man if he
shall gain the whole world and lose his own soul?" Life is
more than success measured by cash or advancement, they
say. They want something both bigger and smaller than a
vice-presidency or an imposing expense account. I have
already mentioned the young doctor I met in my city's most
select hospital—the one who was giving up his chance at
a wealthy practice to do missionary work in Africa. I
could multiply him by twenty even in my limited acquaintance. Everywhere around me the young are disappointing their parents or their employers by vindicating
their ideals. They give up law for furniture-designing ("I
want to make something with my hands"). They resign
from a career in manufacturing for one in teaching ("I
want to use my education"). They throw over a place in
the paternal firm for one in a seminary or a charitable
foundation ("I want to do something for *people*"). Newly
married husbands, and with their wives' approval, uproot
themselves from the city with its high salaries for white-
clapboarded houses in some green village ("where we
won't have much money but we will have some sort of life
for ourselves and our family"). I know a young man who,
after deserting his lucrative advertising job in New York,

moved to a little town in New England and became a salesman for public-school textbooks. "We'll never be rich," he explained to his bewildered parents, "but we don't care about that. Schoolbooks are as necessary to the world as food. It's the one way I can feel *useful*. And our children will know the kind of country life I missed."

They talk a good deal about their children, even before they get them. For this is the philoprogenitive generation. Half a dozen progeny in as many years is not the exception these days but a quite ordinary rule. "A boy for you, a girl for me," the old-fashioned two, is considered a very meager crop indeed.

Their detractors decry even this tendency. They call it obsessive, a retreat into the warm cocoon of domesticity. But what is wrong with such a retreat? No man can live without sanctuary, and this is an honorable one. What is more, young parents pay for their compensations in a very hard-earned coin. Without servants, without the help of spinster aunts or visiting grandmothers (there wouldn't be room for them if they were available), they take on early responsibilities that our generation could scarcely have borne. It is not at all uncommon for a wife in her very early twenties to have three children, the care of an apartment or a house, and a job besides. She also, no doubt, takes part in community activities, paints her kitchen, and cooks like a *cordon bleu*. Her husband, for his part, does his own gardening, repairs his own roof, commutes long hours for the sake of country air at night, and does his civic share in the same community. (I include these busy idealists among the younger set because the pair I visualize are certainly under thirty and very likely closer to twenty-five.)

But is the picture altogether so rosy as I seem to paint? Have the young no limitations? Of course they have. They possess the defects of their qualities, like all mankind, and they still have much to learn. If they are not selfish, they are self-centered, sometimes to an immense degree. If they demand tolerance for suppressed peoples, they are apt to show no tolerance at all toward stupidity or dullness closer to home. "Honor thy Father and thy Mother" seems to them one of the lesser commandments. They are likely to be secretive, aloof, and condescending toward every generation and every tradition except their own. And they are not really lighthearted in the way I remember from my own youth.

How could they be? They have inherited a tilting planet, a dubious future. Boys know they must eventually interrupt their lives for a long tour of military duty. They understand that, taxes being what they are, it will be nearly impossible to build a fortune or pass on a patrimony. The girls realize their burdens will be heavier ones than their mothers or their grandmothers had to carry. So pure frolic vanishes early. They take play as seriously as they do their studies or their employment, and they seem to us morbidly intense. But they are brave and talented and full of fortitude.

Few of them, like our Bridie, will be emigrating. But if

circumstances compelled them, I think they could manage that just as courageously as she. From the seventeen-year-olds crying out, "What have I done with my life?" to the young parents asking soberly, "How can we lead a useful existence?" they are an attractive lot and the hope of the world.

# A Lost Privilege

THERE is a house out of my childhood which I recall with peculiar nostalgia. It did not belong to my own family but to a grand-aunt whom I used occasionally to visit in the summers. Aunt Jeanette was a widow and she had lived—forever, it seemed to me—in an ugly turreted piece of Victoriana with a basement kitchen and a garden primly bedded with salvia and canna lilies. Her benevolences were austere. She had no children and few friends with children, nor did she bother to provide me with much amusement. In that house was no closetful of toys, no conscious device for trapping children's fancies. She let me accompany her shopping and gave me a great deal of lemonade, and I was permitted all the time I liked in the local library; but if there were treats like picnics and excursions I have forgotten them. I remember only that she taught me several different ways of playing solitaire.

I loved that fortnight with Aunt Jeanette, however, for a reason dearer than entertainment, and that was the bedroom where she always let me sleep. It was alone in a cupola. An eccentric, spiraling set of stairs led up to it from the second floor. It had no bathroom near, and only two of its four windows opened. In hot weather it must have been unbearably stuffy for anyone over twelve years old. But it was sweetly, entirely, irresistibly private. No eyes peered in on me, no household voice reached me once I shut the door. I could look out over treetops and imagine myself anything from Rapunzel to the Little Lame Prince. Aunt Jeanette was strict about mealtimes but otherwise tranquil about my non-appearances, and never before or since have I had such a heady sense of being mistress of my own domain.

I always returned home reluctantly, and am not yet able to pass a place of that period without wishing it belonged to me. Recently, in our village, a rococo house went on the market and I rushed around to it at once with the real-estate dealer, plans for remodeling it hot in my head. But its architect had been a cheat. There were no stairs to any aerie, the cupola being nothing but an exterior decoration —literally a hollow sham. So ended my dreams of a tower. I went back to my stubborn daily struggle for a genuine retreat, one unviolated by visitors, maids, progeny, or the telephone.

Now I am quite the opposite of a recluse. I like parties and people, fiercely cherish my friends. I am perfectly willing to put up lodgers for the night, out-of-town guests, relatives, and frequent hordes of young ladies who leave their slippers under every sofa and invite their young men to make themselves free with the refrigerator. But I have never lost my longing for privacy, that most civilized of luxuries, and perhaps the one most difficult to get.

Sometimes I think people have forgotten it *is* a luxury. This is an age which puts a premium on "togetherness," on the extroverted and unprivate soul. From infancy at home, from kindergarten at school, citizens are taught that they must adjust to a public mold. Heads of government are judged as much on their ability to "mingle" as on their gifts of statesmanship. Business expects its executives to have a folksy way with stockholders, be open with the press, and marry wives who conform to an approved gregarious pattern. Anonymity we seem to fear as if, in losing touch with multitudes, we also lose touch with ourselves. It used to be said that a gentleman had his name in the papers only three times in his life—when he was born, when he married, when he died. Now no one seems to mind name or picture published in any medium, complete with the most intimate details. Scotch lords stand for their portraits, praising plaid socks. American families sail on their national steamship lines and approve them all in print. Librettists write musical comedies lampooning female ambassadors or important international marriages, and the living prototypes of their characters are expected to take the matter in good fun. It isn't considered sporting to object to being goldfish.

On the same public plan we build our dwelling places. Where, in many a modern house, can one hide? (And every being, cat, dog, parakeet, or man, wants a hermitage now and then.) We discard partitions and put up dividers. Utility rooms take the place of parlors. Picture windows look not onto seas or mountains or even shrubberies but into the picture windows of the neighbors. Hedges come down, gardens go unwalled; and we have nearly forgotten that the inventor of that door which first shut against intrusion was as much mankind's benefactor as he who discovered fire. I suspect that, in a majority of the bungalows sprouting across the country like toadstools after a rain, the only apartment left for a citadel is the bathroom. In our commendable search for light, air, sunshine, and, of course, economy, privacy has been the chief sacrifice.

Yet who could deny that privacy is a jewel? It has always been the mark of privilege, the distinguishing feature of a truly urbane culture. Out of the cave, the tribal tepee, the pueblo, the community fortress, man emerged to build himself a house of his own with a shelter in it for himself and his diversions. Every age has seen it so. The poor might have to huddle together in cities for need's sake, and the frontiersman cling to his neighbors for the sake of protection. But in each civilization, as it advanced, those who could afford it chose the luxury of a withdrawing-place. Egyptians planned vine-hung gardens, the Greeks had their porticos and seaside villas, the Romans put enclosures around their patios, and English gentlemen retired into their country seats guarded by parks and lime-walks and disciplined stone walls. Privacy was considered as worth striving for as hallmarked silver or linen sheets to one's bed.

Then why, in this country of abundance, have we undervalued it? The miracle of our culture is that so many graces which once only the very rich could enjoy have been made available to all, or nearly all. Only the great man once had his own carriage. It was the privileged few who ate fruit out of season, traveled to foreign parts, could keep warm in winter and clean at any time of year. Now two hundred horses carry the artisan to his work, and he likely dines on beefsteak and salad and strawberry shortcake, as if he were a gourmet, any January evening. Everybody—or nearly everybody—can read and write, buy a book, take holidays, play golf, sail boats, own an overcoat, and see a play on television every night. Dishes get washed by electricity; the sick get medicine. Bodies and even souls have more cosseting than ever before in history. Nobody starves—except for a place to be happily solitary.

But starvation of the spirit is as real as bodily famine. It's all very well to talk about man's need to communicate and to own affection. A spate of books and psychiatric papers, of essays and lectures and solemn dissertations, have pontificated on it. We weep for those who do not belong, shed tears for the Outsider. "Love or perish" we are told and we tell ourselves. The phrase is true enough so long as we do not interpret it as "Mingle or be a failure." Loving our neighbor should not mean that we must sit on his lap. It does not mean having no respite from him. A friend is not an eavesdropper, a devoted parent does not force confidences, and the more intimate a family circle, the more fresh air and mental breathing-space that circle should enclose. The human animal needs a freedom seldom mentioned, freedom from intrusion. He needs a little privacy quite as much as he wants understanding or vitamins or exercise or praise.

I remember my cupola as others remember the treehouses or tents or abandoned piano boxes of their childhoods. I never had another nook quite so desirable. But I do look back kindly to a time, not so long ago, when a sort of accidental gift came my way. Again it was in the summer. My daughters were at camp. The cook was on vacation. And quite unexpectedly my husband was called out of town. For five days (the first in many years) I was completely and blissfully unsurrounded. No voices called me from upstairs or down. I had nobody to urge or soothe or mollify or exhort or pick up after. I was no one's social secretary, adviser, nurse, or menu-consultant. What did I do with my leisure? I don't believe I did anything. I did not work; I telephoned no friends. I refused all offers of dinners, treats, and company. In a daze of privacy I wandered about the house, ate when I thought of it, basked in silence as if it had been sun. One day I didn't even dress. Although I was in perfectly good health, I felt languid as a convalescent. And perhaps I was one, recovering from eighteen or twenty seasons of domestic pressures. I loafed, and if I did not exactly invite my soul, it came back to me uninvited. I was happy to see my dears return, and have felt since no urge to repeat the experience. But I recall it tenderly.

And this in spite of the fact that we are rather a private

race as families go. We respect one another's personalities and would rather cut our throats than read one another's letters. If our house is not new, it is commodious. No one needs to share a bedroom, and there are bathrooms enough to go around. The television sits in an apartment of its own so that it impinges on no life except that of the viewer. We have desks that lock, doors that shut. Nobody overlooks our garden. Yet I evidently needed pause from even my share of public living. How must it go, then, with wives and husbands and children thrown together, constantly higgledy-piggledy in the closeness of modern subdivisions? How do they endure the walls that can be heard through, the community laundries, the areas that must be library-nursery-parlor-conservatory-study, all at once? Why, with fortitude and gritted teeth, I expect, while they wait for genius to contrive them something to use instead of space and money.

Privacy still comes high. But candles and salt and silk stockings and white bread used to also. We have invented cheap fires, inexpensive cars, labor-savers for the millions. We have cut down on drudgery and made a start on eliminating even poverty itself. We know how to create ersatz furs and pearls and immunities from diseases. Surely something can be done to design for us all an acceptable substitute for a Victorian cupola.

# The Consolations of Illiteracy

THERE is something to be said for a bad education. By any standards mine was deplorable; and I deplored it for years, in private and in public. I flaunted it as if it were a medal, a kind of cultural Purple Heart which both excused my deficiencies and lent luster to my mild achievements. But as time goes on I murmur against it less. I find that even ignorance has its brighter side.

For if I grew up no better instructed about the world of books than was Columbus about global geography, I had in store for me, as he did, the splendors of discovery. There is such a thing as a literary landscape; to that, to nearly the whole length and breadth of classic English writing, I came as an astonished stranger. No one who first enters that country on a conducted tour can have any notion what it is like to travel it alone, on foot, and at his own pace.

I am not exaggerating. My education really was bad. As a child I lived on a ranch in Colorado with the nearest one-room schoolhouse four miles away and the roads nearly impassable in winter. Sometimes there was no teacher for the school; sometimes my brother and I were the only pupils. If there was a public library within practical distance I never learned of it. We were a reading family but my father's library ran chiefly to history and law and the collected works of Bulwer-Lytton. I wolfed down what I could but found a good deal of it indigestible. In my teens neither the public high school of a very small Western town nor the decorous boarding school I later attended made much effort to mend the damage. It seems to me now that we were always having to make reports on *Ivanhoe* or repeat from memory passages from Burke's *Speech on Conciliation*. I think in two separate English classes we spent most of the year parsing "Snowbound."

However, it was at college I seriously managed to learn nothing. My alma mater was one of those universities founded and supplied by the state which in the West everybody attends as automatically as kindergarten. There are—or were then—no entrance examinations. Anybody could come and everybody did, for the proms and the football games; and they sat under a faculty which for relentless mediocrity must have outstripped any in the land. So, by putting my mind to it, I was able to emerge from four years there quite uncorrupted by knowledge. Let me amend that to literary knowledge. Somewhere along the line, out of a jumble of courses in Sociology, Household Chemistry, Hygiene, Beginner's German, I remember picking up bits and pieces of learning designed to enrich my life: the Theory of Refrigeration; the fact that Old German and Anglo-Saxon were two languages balefully akin and equally

revolting; and the law about no offspring's having eyes
darker than the eyes of the darker of his two parents. I had
also, in one semester, been made to bolt Shakespeare entire, including the sonnets; and the result of such forced
feeding had left me with an acute allergy to the Bard I was
years getting over. Otherwise, few Great Books had im-
pinged on my life. Through a complicated system of jug-
gling credits and wheedling heads of departments, I had
been able to evade even the Standard General Survey of
English Literature.

I had read things, of course. I was even considered quite
a bookworm by my sorority sisters, who had given up going
to the library after polishing off *The Wizard of Oz*. But
it was the contemporaries who occupied me. I had read
Mencken but not Marlowe, Atherton but not Austen,
Hoffenstein but not Herrick, Shaw but not Swift, Kipling
but not Keats, Millay but not Marvell. Unbelievable as it
may seem to an undergraduate, I had never even read A. E.
Housman. Although I had scribbled verses in my note-
books during geology lectures, I had not so much as heard
of Herbert or Donne or Gay or Prior or Hopkins. I had
shunned Chaucer and avoided Dryden. Oliver Goldsmtih
I knew by hearsay as the author of a dull novel called *The
Vicar of Wakefield*. Milton had written solely in order to
plague the young with "Il Penseroso." I hadn't read *Vanity Fair* or *Ethan Frome* or "Essay on Man" or *Anna
Karenina* or "The Hound of Heaven" or *Dubliners*. (Joyce
was a contemporary but the furore over *Ulysses* was a mist
that obscured his younger work.) Almost none of the al-

leged classics, under whose burden the student is supposed to bow, had I peered into either for pleasure or for credit.

As a consequence, although I came to them late, I came to them without prejudice. We met on a basis completely friendly; and I do not think the well-educated can always claim as much.

I commiserate, indeed, with people for whom *Silas Marner* was once required reading. They tell me it left permanent scars on their childhood; and I am certain they could not approach George Eliot as open-mindedly as I did, only a year or two ago, when I tried *Adam Bede* as one might try for the first time an olive. "But it's magnificent!" I went around exclaiming to my friends. "I've been deceived! You told me George Eliot was dull."

I pity the unlucky ones who wrote compositions on "Richardson as the Father of the English Novel." They could never come, relaxed and amused, upon *Pamela* as if it were a brand-new book. The literate may cherish as dearly as I do such disparate joys as "The Deserted Village" or *Pride and Prejudice* or *The Old Curiosity Shop* or *The Bostonians*. I do not think, however, they feel the same proprietary delight as I do toward them. Behind those pages, for me, hovers no specter of the classroom and the loose-leaf notebook. Each is my own discovery.

Often such discoveries have been embarrassing. Once I had begun to read for pleasure in a century not my own, I kept stumbling across treasures new to me only. I remember when I first pulled *Cranford* out of a boarding-house bookcase shortly after I had left college. For weeks I kept buttonholing my friends to insist they taste with me that remarkable and charming tidbit written by some unheard-of wit who signed herself simply "Mrs. Gaskell." And I recall how I blushed to learn they had nearly all read it—and disliked it—as juniors. Although I no longer go about beating the drum for each masterpiece I unearth, neither am I apologetic about someone's having been there before me. After all, Cortez (or Balboa, if one insists on being literal) must have known, when he surveyed the Pacific from that peak in Darien, that generations of Indians had seen it earlier. But the view was new to him. His discovery was important because it came at the right time in his career.

So mine have come. There are books that one needs maturity to enjoy just as there are books an adult can come on too late to savor. I have never, for instance, been able to get through *Wuthering Heights*. That I should have read before I was sixteen. I shall never even *try Treasure Island*, which I missed at twelve.

On the other hand, no child can possibly appreciate *Huckleberry Finn*. That is not to say he can find no pleasure in it. He can and does. But it takes a grownup to realize its wry and wonderful bouquet. Imagine opening it for the first time at forty! That was my reward for an underprivileged youth. For that Mark Twain shall have my heart and hand forever, in spite of what he said about Jane Austen. "It's a pity they let her die a natural death," he wrote to William Dean Howells. Perhaps the young Samuel Clemens read her as part of a prescribed curriculum. Otherwise how could even that opinionated and undereducated genius have so misjudged an ironic talent more towering than his own? Had I been younger than thirty when I first happened on Miss Austen I might have found her dry. Had I read her much later I might have been too dry myself. Her season suited me.

For no matter how enchanting to the young are the realms of gold, maturity makes one a better traveler there. Do not misunderstand me. I wish with all my heart that I had taken to the road earlier; I do not boast because I was provincial so long. But since I began the journey late, I make use of what advantages I have. So, for one thing, I capitalize on my lack of impatience. I am not on fire to see everything at once. There is no goal I must reach by any sunset. And how fresh all the landscape is to me! I wander as far afield as I care to; one range of hills opens out into another which I shall explore in due time. I move forward or backward. I retrace my steps when I please. I fall in love with the formal grandeur of the eighteenth century and stop there for as many months as the mood holds. Boswell's *London Journal* leads me back into Johnson himself and into the whole great age. I read Pope and Gray and Goldsmith and backward still through Richardson and Fielding. I read the letters and diaries of Miss Burney because Dr. Johnson calls her his "dear little Fanny." (The view there is unimportant but amusing.) And that leads me forward once more to Jane Austen. I could not proceed at a pace so leisurely were I twenty once more and in haste to keep up with the fashionable cults. I go where I like. I read Gibbon one week and Sarah Orne Jewett the next, with catholic pleasure. Henry James entertains me not because he is in the mode but because he is enthralling, and I continue to prefer *The Bostonians* to *The Golden Bowl*. I do not need to praise Kafka; and I can keep Montaigne and Clarence Day and Coleridge on the same bedside stand.

Because I am grown-up I am under no compulsion from either the critics or the professors to like *anything*. If I try *Tristram Shandy* and find it heavy going, I admit it and never open the second volume. If I do not agree with the world that *Moby Dick* is the Great American Novel, studded with the richest possible symbolism, I need not pretend to enjoy Melville. I think Trollope dull. That is nothing against Trollope; I need not dwell in the country he has invented.

And it is wonderful to be a member of no party! I pick my own way among the landmarks. No Baedeker distracts me from the scenery. I can be behind-times enough to like Tennyson and Browning. I can prefer Crashaw to Donne and Willa Cather to Ronald Firbank. I can read (and disagree with) Virginia Woolf on Monday and on Tuesday begin an amiable argument with Newman; nor do I find it a dizzy flight. And so much still to see! Peak upon peak unfolds. But there are also delightful little fenced fields and flowery culverts where I can rest when I do not wish to climb. I have not yet read *War and Peace*. But then I've never read anything by Rider Haggard, either, or Wilkie Collins, or anything of Mary Webb's except *Precious*

*Bane*. I haven't read Pepys's Diary or Katherine Mansfield's. I have *The House of the Seven Gables* ahead of me, and I have also *Our Mutual Friend*.

For of all my discoveries, nearly the most breathless was Dickens himself. How many of the educated can even suspect the delights of such a delayed encounter? I think we owned a *Collected Works* when I was a child. But I had tried *David Copperfield* too early and had believed all my life that he was not for me. One night last winter I was sleepless and somehow without a book. From our own shelves I took down *Little Dorrit*, which people tell me now is one of the least beguiling of the lot. But Keats first looking on his Homer could have been no more dazzled than I first poring on my Boz. I felt as a treasure-hunter might feel had he tripped over the locked chest that belonged to Captain Kidd. "Oh, my America, my new-found land!" How many novels were there? Thirty-odd? And every one of them still to be possessed! I got as drunk on Dickens for a while as I used to on the Cavalier poets when I first discovered *them*. I read, in quick succession, *Great Expectations, Martin Chuzzlewit, Oliver Twist, The Pickwick Papers,* the very *David Copperfield* which had once put me off, and then the preposterous, magnificent, exasperating, ridiculous, and utterly engrossing *Bleak House*. I stopped there for fear I should have a surfeit; but it's consoling to know the rest of the novels are there waiting for me, none of them grown stale or too familiar for enjoyment.

There is still much to deplore about my education. I

shall never read Latin verse in the original or have a taste for the Brontës, and those are crippling lacks. But all handicaps have compensations, and I have learned to accept both cheerfully. To have first met Dickens, Austen, and Mark Twain when I was capable of giving them the full court curtsy is beatitude enough for any reader. Blessed are the illiterate, for they shall inherit the Word!

*Frivolities*

# How to Get Along with Men

NOTHING fails like success; nothing is so defeated as yesterday's triumphant Cause. I think often and with pity of those old Feminist ghosts who won their battles but lost their war. They must be giddy with spinning in their graves. For their daughters and their granddaughters— freedom secure, their shackles burst—have been the meanest of traitors. They have run merrily back to their chains.

Now that girls need not marry for financial security, they marry younger and more eagerly than before. Now that limiting the size of a family requires no esoteric knowledge, the families get bigger and bigger to the despair of school systems and Margaret Sanger. In spite of (or perhaps because of) Birds-Eye-begotten dinners and the world's fruits in Cellophane, nearly all of us are better cooks than our ancestresses. The New Woman has turned out to be romantically domestic. I know women who grind their own coffee, preserve their own peaches, bake their own bread, grow their own herbs. Almost any day I expect to find certain accomplished friends of mine out in their vineyards, treading their own grapes.

So it's not astonishing that in this age of clear-eyed, emancipated youth, the world is fuller than ever of tracts directed at its distaff section—is brimful of recipes for pleasing gentlemen and ensnaring spouses. Even the most ambitious careerist now admits that a husband is vital to her whole scheme of things; that the proper study of womankind is Men.

But I sometimes think the pundits have got hold of the wrong end of the stick. Capturing male fancy isn't all that difficult. Though it can't be taught by rote any more than absolute pitch, nine-tenths of the girl babies born into the world have the gift perfected by the time they are drinking out of a cup. I recall a demonstration of native talent given by a member of my own household when she was four and out with me for a Sunday call. We must have dropped in at cocktail time, for there were present a large number of grownups. And, when the moment came to go, she detached her hand from mine, walked all the way across the room to the tallest and likeliest male stranger, and murmured meltingly, "Will you tie my bonnet for me?"

I decided then and there that whatever crumbs of counsel on How to Deal with the Other Sex I'd been hoarding, I'd keep them for my memoirs.

If all girls do not play the music thus by ear, they've usually learned, by eighteen, at least to carry the tune. They've learned from their sisters and schoolmates, by trial and error, from exhortations in their own glossy magazines. Besides being all beautiful as nymphs—hair shining, teeth flashing like pearls or kitchen porcelain, complexions incorrigibly perfect—they have studied how to take an intelligent interest in whatever interests their prey. If need be, they can ski down terrible mountains, reef a sail, or listen interminably to the sound of locomotives on hi-fi. They are abetted, moreover, by the passion for marrying which has infected even men. Never has bachelorhood been so little at a premium. So it's an egregious female nowadays who does not, in due course, acquire a husband. One or several.

Which brings me to the root of my particular matter. Getting along with men isn't what's truly important. The vital knowledge is how to get along with a man, one man. And concerning that I think our mothers and our grandmothers knew more than we.

For one thing, they recognized their luck. They never stopped preening themselves on having the good fortune to be married women. I fear the feminists have had their little victory after all. They've persuaded us that marriage is a partnership, with inflexible rights and guarantees, and that the price of feminine freedom is eternal vigilance—on our own behalf. Nonsense! Marriage is a lot of things—an alliance, a sacrament, a comedy, or a mistake; but it is definitely not a partnership because that implies equal gain. And every right-thinking woman knows the profit in matrimony is by all odds hers. Simone de Beauvoir, the French humorist, wrote a very funny book a few years ago (at least I laughed at it a good bit). What amused me most was her insistence that men had invented marriage to keep women in their places as the Second Sex. Now why would a man deliberately go out of his way to dream up an institution so hampering to his liberty, so chafing to the wild male spirit, and above all so expensive? The wheel, yes; the moon-bound rocket; even Scotch Tape. But marriage was all a woman's idea, and for man's acceptance of the pretty yoke it becomes us to be grateful.

If ever I were intrepid enough to instruct my daughters on the care and taming of husbands, I should put gratitude first on my list.

Perhaps it need be the only comment there. For gratitude is a sincerer form of flattery than imitation; and for its sake a man will endure a great deal—will bear with extravagance, too much marjoram in casseroles, or a tendency to sinus trouble. It is better than charity at covering a multitude of faults.

Faults there are bound to be, marked, like towels, plainly His and Hers. But the woman who gets along with a man knows how to get along also with his defects. She is too sensible to try to erase them, so she adopts them. The most successfully married couples I know have, perhaps unconsciously, worked this out; and so I shall remark to my daughters. Is the lord of the manor unpunctual about letters or meeting one at the station? Does he drink too much coffee, clutter ash trays, read late at night in bed, turn on all the lights and leave them burning? Is he a pantry-raider, an ice-tray emptier, careless of calories? Does he tramp in gardening boots across the Saturday carpet and think one's old boarding-school friends are bores? Let it not exacerbate the soul. Be unpunctual together. Let the lights burn and the leaves gather on the rug and the ice melt in the sink. See old cronies at lunch without him or suffer them less gladly. Faults shared are comfortable as bedroom slippers and as easy to slip into. I have a feeling that Darby and his Joan were probably both terrible housekeepers and ramshackle hosts, but that Joan kept a pot of coffee—or was it mead?— ready at all times for the two of them. And I'll wager she laughed heartily at every joke he told while they were tucking it away.

For next to gratitude, and ornamenting it, I should put appreciation. Particularly appreciation of his wit. A husband expects a certain amount of disillusionment. He knows that a helpmate before breakfast is bound to be less picturesque than the *soignée* creature with whom he danced at the Assemblies. He has braced himself for hair nets and flannel bathrobes! What he hasn't counted on is a wife who either interrupts his newest Madison Avenue jape with, "You'll have to call the carpenters, honey, about that storm window," or greets its point with a chill stare.

Nor is he prepared at parties to have her snatch the same story away from him and finish it herself. Perhaps half the wife-murders in history would have gone uncommitted if the murderee had not, at some time during a convivial evening, stopped her husband dead in the middle of a story with an impatient, "Oh, Harry, you're getting it all wrong! The dog doesn't come in till later. You see there were these two sailors . . ."

I happen to be married, myself, to a genuine wit; I *know* that his most offhand dinner-table observation is far funnier than anything Abe Burrows ever said, and it makes for an agreeable life. But a good many husbands might be coruscating at dinner too, if they were nicely applauded.

Let's see—that's three items on the list and it seems very skimpy advice for a woman to have accumulated after more than twenty years. My daughters would laugh at me, and quite rightly, if I handed them this trio of tenets. What about the hot meal at night and the good breakfast? What about being tactful to the president of his company? Is there to be no sound counsel on staying slimly seductive, on asking intelligent business questions, on Getting One's Way without a Fuss?

I'd have to admit I was a poor oracle. I've seen marriages fly apart at the seams and I've seen them firmly welded as a battleship, and there was never a rule of thumb to go by. Good housekeepers come to grief and bad ones prosper; but I have also seen Craig's wife enthroned like Hera in Mr. Craig's heart. I know happy women who understand more about business than their husbands and equally happy ones who think a Dow-Jones average has something to do with golf. For my part, I suspect the more distance a wife puts between herself and the head of her husband's firm the better; but *Fortune* magazine some years ago found for the opposition.

As for glamour, even that is moot. There's a friend of mine who, although she can scarcely make out the name on a restaurant marquee, leaves her glasses at home because her husband thinks they are unbecoming, and *she's* happy. I also know a witty woman novelist who buttons her sweaters unevenly and forgets her lipstick, and *her* husband hasn't spoken a cross word to her in years. There are executive-type women who do the driving in the family and who replace the fuses and beard the furnace in its den; and then there are the ones—like me—who go into trauma when faced with an automatic pencil sharpener. We all seem to fare about the same. And when it came to the final question, I'd have no answer at all. In a successful marriage, there is no such thing as one's way. There is only the way of both, only the bumpy, dusty, difficult, but always mutual path.

Pressed, I might add two trifles so old-fashioned as to seem fresh. I wish that every girl who marries might have a dot. Not a fortune—that might unbalance a relationship. But the woman with a little money of her own, a bit of change in her pocketbook which is not part of the domestic budget, is delightfully situated. It gives her confidence and kindness, like having naturally curly hair. It might be hers by inheritance. She might earn it by ingenuity. Or she might persuade her husband to delegate some small portion of his monthly stipend to her personal account. Even ten or fifteen dollars a year that was assuredly hers, something with which to buy a hat or a birthday gift (and no questions asked) could make the difference between resentful dependence and happy self-reliance.

The other concerns the selection of a proper family tree. Nothing helps so much in getting along with a man as seeing to it that he stems from a long line of monogamous ancestors.

And there the list would have to end. Gratitude, an attentive ear, a sharing of faults; pocket money and a stout conviction that marriages were meant to last—those are the only recipes I have to offer. I hope no man sees the meager roster, for it might seem to him condescending. And condescension is the poorest weapon in a woman's arsenal. But then, I and my kind do not own an arsenal, having no need of one. Who wants weapons when she has—and is aware that she has—all the luck?

# Pipeline and Sinker

"ALL happy families," said Tolstoi, "resemble one another; every unhappy family is unhappy in its own fashion." Like the generalities of many a lesser sage, the old master's observation has just a trace of truth in it. But not the whole truth. Happiness puts on as many shapes as discontent, and there is nothing odder than the satisfactions of one's neighbor.

Happy families do, however, own a surface similarity of good cheer. For one thing, they like each other, which is quite a different thing from loving. For another, they have, almost always, one entirely personal treasure—a sort of purseful of domestic humor which they have accumulated against rainy days. This humor is not necessarily witty. The jokes may be incomprehensible to outsiders, and the laughter spring from the most trivial of sources. But the jokes and the laughter belong entirely to the families and hence are valuable.

Our own family is probably no gayer than any other group of four people who enjoy each other's company. Still, we have all lived together a long time, and our purse is well supplied. We are forever reaching into it for an anecdote or a recollection.

"Do you remember?" we are continually asking one another.

"Do you remember the picnic when a horse ate our lunch? Do you remember how Daddy always dressed up in a white coat and tied a towel around his head when he took our temperatures? Do you remember the treasure hunt when everybody forgot where we'd hidden the treasure?"

"Khrushchev" is not a funny name but we never hear it without smiling because that is what Patsy used to call her kerchief when she was four. No one ever remarks that a friend's phone is tied up, without our harking back to Julie's first invented witticism at three. On her toy telephone she was intently dialing a number.

"Hello," she said, "is this the zoo? I want to speak to the lion."

There was a suitable silence. Then, turning to me, she said solemnly, "The lion is busy."

We carefully preserve an Easter card which Patsy drew and painted for us when she was perhaps six. There had been a bad drought that spring and she had heard much about being sparing with the water supply. The card was a masterpiece of mingled pagan and religious art—rabbits competing for importance with crosses and lilies. It was given to us folded over like a book, and inside she had drawn three balloons, each with its appropriate legend. The first exclaimed, "Happy Easter!" The second announced that "Christ is Risen!" The third said simply, "Save Water."

When the girls were small we were wary about quoting their sayings. Children do not like to be laughed at. Now, though, they listen greedily when we remind them of unconscious mots from their youth. After all, it is not everyone who can so well sum up the difficulties of virtuous behavior as did our youngest one night at table. We had been discussing, of all things (and we have always discussed all things), saints. We were claiming favorites among them.

"Which saint would you like best to be?" we asked her, expecting the usual platitudes about the vivacious Theresa or the modest Clare. But our child had a mind of her own.

"Oh," she said firmly, "I'd choose to be a martyr."

We evidently gaped, unbelieving; but she had her reasons marshaled. "You see you only have to be a martyr once."

Some of our favorite stories have a pathetic overtone, like clown's comedy; and I dare not name which daughter it was who, in second grade, found a dollar bill in a vacant lot on the way home from school. Honest creature that she was, she went up and down the block for an hour, knocking on each door to inquire if anyone had lost a fortune. We live in an evidently scrupulous village, so no one claimed it, and she brought the dollar proudly home to tuck into her bank. After having reassured her that finders of such anonymous wealth were certainly keepers, I asked, "Did you ever find any money before this?"

"Oh, yes," she told me, "once I found a dime under a tree. But I put it back."

No wonder I still worry about that child, even now that she is grown-up.

The whole family laughs at me, but not at my jokes, which are rare. What they recall most hilariously are the scrapes I get into through my total lack of mechanical ability. They stopped commenting on the fact I can't cope with a pencil sharpener or efficiently defrost a refrigerator. They no longer expect me to read a road map or assemble a food chopper. But when I once got locked for hours into my stall shower by pulling the shower door straight through the jamb instead of pushing it properly out—a feat of idiot strength unparalleled by Atlas—it kept them happy as crickets. Particularly when they learned that the handyman from the house next to us had to take the door off its hinges to release me (after someone had mercifully tossed a dressing gown over the transom).

It is my husband, though, whose wit we chiefly savor.

"Here comes Daddy," Julie sang out once when she was a very small girl, waiting at the corner of the hedge for her commuting ancestor. "He brings fun! He brings joy! He brings the paper!"

The compliment with a sting in its tail is our copyrighted brand of family humor. But she was a wise child. She knew her own parent and realized even so early that a cheerful father is as important as he is rare. My husband's jests will not make a Hollywood fortune. Bennett

Cerf will never collect his pearls for a column. *We* collect them, though, and tell our beads with mirth.

I have said in another connection that he is a wit and I stand by that. He is not, however, a raconteur. He has no patience with a manufactured joke and is as likely to betray the point of one by telling it backwards as he is to coin a personal epigram. At those, in our minds, he excels.

"Children should be herded but not seen," he instructed our first nursemaid, quite untruthfully. And he asked me once plaintively why the young must "always run downstairs at the tops of their voices?"

"I have a phenomenal memory," he told a friend of ours who boasted of his steel-trap mind. "I can forget anything."

We do not disdain puns in our limited circle, and we still delight in the social criticism he let fly one evening at the theater. The occasion was a theater benefit for a Worthwhile Charity, but Charity turned out to be very dressy indeed, the orchestra full of white ties and strapless gowns. "Don't you think," he asked me between acts, "that this is rather putting on the underdog?"

And, social or not, I have always cherished his comment on an exceedingly broken-down Victorian chair which I brought home from an auction. "Ah," he said appreciatively, "custom-built, no doubt, for the Hunchback of Notre Dame."

Yet it is not his conscious but rather his unpremeditated witticisms which we most greedily collect. For this is a man impatient with the confines of language. Words get in his way, and he meets them head-on, whereat the words obligingly telescope themselves into charming—and apt—portmanteaus. "Dwelf" is ever so much better than "dwarf" or even "elf," we believe, as a description of something gnomish.

"And I fell for it," I heard him murmur after one of the girls had brought off a teasing coup. "Fell for it—pipeline and sinker."

"She's dumb as the ace of spades," he says. Or, "The poor man hasn't a frog's chance."

"I'm so tired I can't keep open" may have a peculiar sound, but how completely fitting it is to describe a state of enervation. We repeat it after him with relish. And we like the way he described a recent acquisition of the household. Dido, our savage but beautiful black cat (named for the Carthaginian queen) was suddenly a mother. My husband rejoiced. He likes cats. He came up from a look at the new nursery, beaming and too enthusiastic to rummage through his vocabulary for the exact word. What he invented was far more expressive. "There she is, proud as Lucifer," he told us, "with that batter of kittens swirming around her." Certainly batter is a splendid term for kittens and "swirming" which must be a combination of "squirming" and "swarming" has elements of genius.

Our favorite, though, is a simple sentence of gratitude. Someone, one broiling day in the garden, brought him a cold drink.

"Thanks," he exclaimed appreciatively after he had downed it. "That was absolutely a Godsaver."

But if we admire the unexpected rather more than we do his formal japes, we also cherish his description of a certain gossip as "living from mouth to mouth" and of a critic we know as "earning his bread in the sweat of his highbrow." And we never take a motoring trip together that we do not keep in mind his deathless admonition: "We're in a hurry. We haven't time to take a short cut."

If it is true, as he once misquoted Thoreau, that "The mass of men live lives of quiet exasperation," then such recollections as these are the balm.

I have been dipping into the purse at random. The supply is nearly limitless, but many of the happenings which in memory cause us most mirth would not stir anyone but us. These are private treats, privately arrived at. Half of them depend on the joy of recognition. Some of them are esoteric as runes.

Which reminds me of the first time "esoteric" became a family joke. I must explain that, at post-kindergarten age, Pat liked to consider herself never an outsider to anything. "Yes, I know" was the phrase oftenest on her tongue, whether we were discussing modern art, gardening, or child psychology. She was also old enough to be interested in words but young enough to take them literally.

"Your father makes esoteric jokes," I once remarked at dinner.

"What does *that* mean?" she demanded promptly.

"Esoteric?" I said, always happy to inform the young

idea. "Oh, that refers to something private or hidden, something," I went on, "which is known to only a few people."

"Yes, I know," she said automatically.

There was a brief pause, and then came her station announcement. "Yes, I do know. And I know the people, too."

Perhaps it's knowing the people which gives a jest its finest flavor.

# Against Gardens

IT IS ten o'clock on a Saturday morning in Spruce Manor, our flowery suburb. The month is May, the sun is shining, and the air smells sweet of lilac and lily of the valley and Weed Killer 2-4-D. Outside the windows of the kitchen, where my husband and I are lazily pouring ourselves a cup of coffee, we see the world at work—the bee raiding the hyacinth, the robin advancing on the worm, all our soil-colored, grass-stained neighbors in their regular week-end fury of pruning, snipping, dividing, spraying, heeling-in, grubbing out, and propping up. Automatically my husband reaches as if for his gardening shears. I shake my head warningly, whereat he relaxes and butters another slice of toast.

For this year the Saturday fever is not for us. After eighteen years we are giving up a habit as wasteful as drink, nearly as obsessive as drugs. We are now charter members in good standing of Horticulturists Anonymous, Local Chapter Number 1; reformed addicts in the process of reducing our garden to not much more than a "green thought in a green shade."

[ 87 ]

Later in the morning we will perhaps give the lawn-mower a brisk spin. We may even lean across the fence to commend the man next door, whose peonies show such prosperous buds. But we will not linger too long at any such outdoor pastime. Since we can't take it calmly, we're leaving it alone.

Not that we do not love gardens or know how to make them. We love them as alcoholics love the martini. And we are wise with the lore of eighteen studious years. We know all the triumphs, all the crosses—from Achillea and Aphid to Zinnia elegans (dust with light sulphur). We know cold-frames and burlap wrapping, how it feels to see one's own crocus pushing through the snow earlier than any other crocus in the village. We know the dubious delights of raising perennials from seed; and we understand the treacheries of slug, squirrel, rabbit, mole, black spot, blotch, blister beetle, menatodes, and roadside nurserymen. On our half-acre we have planted and frequently seen flourish nearly every flower, shrub, and vegetable likely to thrive in our uncertain climate—and some not so likely. We have mulched and weeded and hoed and been elated and cast down. We have tended trees and experimented with wild flowers. The uses of bone-meal, Vigoro, sheep manure, bucket pumps, and Bordeaux Mixture are no mystery to us. And our decision to make away with blossom and vegetable is due not to disappointment but to success.

For we found ourselves, seven months of the year, slaves

to our bit of property. Sometimes, if we were working with winter bloom, it was twelve.

As slaves, we were willing enough. Gardening has compensations out of all proportion to its goals. It is creation in the pure sense. That dungareed figure scrabbling in the earth, with dirt under his fingernails and thorn scratches on his arms, is no figure of fun but half a god. The sun beats on him, the rain wets him, arthritis lurks under his kneeling pad, ants run up and down his sleeves. Still, it is the posture and the task he dotes on. To be able to walk about a border after dinner and smell the fragrances of his verbena, to speak a personal word to each painted daisy; to pull up a wild onion or congratulate the tuberous begonia he has steered past the nursery stage and into preposterous flower—those are pleasures past explaining. But pleasure can turn into dissipation, as we found to our expense.

The beginning, of course, was all hopeful delight. We were early in the trend to the suburbs, early in the now common pattern of a young couple without much money saved, who buy a house in an upper-middle-class area and yearn to make the earth blossom like a Jackson and Perkins Hybrid Perpetual Climbing Rose.

The house *we* bought was an elderly one, and it already had a garden of sorts, running chiefly to cedar planting and effete narcissi. "So much green," we said, pouting. "No color, no plan. What lack of imagination!"

Our own imaginations were vivid enough for three fam-

ilies. We knew what we wanted, what is wanted today by
half the young people moving into new homes: a small
estate, complete to borders, beddings, herbs, nine bean
rows, and maybe a honey bee. Nor were we entire novices.
My husband, particularly, bragged of a thumb so green
that he could use it for a safety signal. Had he not, in our
city apartment, forced amaryllis into almost obscene
growth? Had he not gained a certain dubious fame for the
corn he once grew on a rooftop in Brooklyn Heights—
seven stunted but recognizable ears? I had lent a hand at
home in our Western garden and remembered tying sweet
peas and watering four-o'clocks. (Whatever happened to
four-o'clocks, by the way? I never see them. They must
have died out like the passenger pigeon.)

So we made our dreams come true in glorious Tech-
nicolor. After we had classified and explored—after we
had picked up the sticks, stones, tin cans, and buried bones
and pushed back the jungle, we moved in with the zeal of
the True Believer. We built frames. We nursed seedlings
and slips. We laid out borders for perennials and beds for
annuals. We studied the tedious techniques of transplant-
ing, grafting, naturalizing, and massing for effect. And
crops grew for us obediently. We had the tallest digitalis
and the finest cup-and-saucer flowers, the most sentimental
bleeding hearts and the tinkliest coral bells of any garden
in town. Anchusa or columbine, veronica or flax, sweet
rocket, snow-in-summer, sundrops, larkspur, scabiosa, sweet
alyssum—they were all ours at one time or another. We
stole lady's-slipper and Jack-in-the-pulpit from the woods,

and they took kindly to the shade of the rhododendron. Passers-by used to exclaim over our lilies, and the neighbors envied the showiness of our double stock. We grew herbs. We grew broccoli. Every year we added or changed or enlarged—at a cost of money and effort which only the devotee would believe.

In order to buy laurel for hedging and trumpet vines for our expensive split-rail fence, we gave up summer trips. We stayed away from the theater so that we could afford a novel front walk which would be a combination of rock garden and shrubbery. When it came to a choice between new clothes and a pair of holly trees (for holly has to have a mate, like a lovebird) or rare new hybrids, we thought there *was* no choice. Clothes became unimportant, anyhow. We had no time to visit friends, and who can go out to dine with eternally earth-stained hands? Part of the time we couldn't have even straightened up enough to be guests at anyone's table. Our backs took on permanent curves from continual crouching in search of a weed in the garden or a dandelion in the lawn.

For the trouble with gardening, I repeat, is that it does not remain an avocation. It becomes an obsession.

I don't refer to those undedicated souls who throw a few seeds into a back-yard patch and hope for the best; or who do their landscaping with marigolds. The real devotee will filch the money for his wife's winter coat and spend it on a new breed of gladiolus. He will dip into principal and send his children for their working papers before he will relinquish the double pink Dutch hyacinths he has on order at his jobbers'. For the sake of his dwarf dahlias or a new strain of tea rose, he will drive his old car past the safety margin, forgo painting the house, and eat casseroles in lieu of steak. He will water illegally in droughts, quarrel with his neighbor over marauding dogs, and forget about that Maine motoring trip because there is so much work to do around the place. He is vassal, not lord, of his land, and at the mercy of all his enemies.

His enemies are legion. Take birds, for instance. Whose heart is so hard it does not melt to hear the twittering of wrens at their front doors, the song of thrush and robin? Whose eye is so blind to beauty that it does not follow joyfully the flash of a blue jay's wing through spring sky? The gardener's, for one. Birds are both his allies and his foes. They fly off with labels and ties. They eat up his grass seed. His trees, his vines, his fruits are quite literally for them. We found blueberry bushes on our property, but we have never found the berries. We own a cherry tree, which we share—one pie for us, a summer's larder for them. We once spent all our week ends and half the roof-repairs money on cheesecloth with which to net the fruit. We didn't know, then, that birds could *climb*. But there we saw them, every fine day, perched inside the netting, devouring our incipient preserves.

Squirrels take the walnuts and the corn. Dogs bury bones among the snapdragon and play tag in the geraniums. Rabbits are fond of lupins and of lettuces. Small boys trudge through cutting beds on their way to school. For every flower there is a blight and for every vegetable a parasite or a disease. But nothing quite equals in destructive force one species of enemy not always recognized as such. I refer to the Angel of Death or Professional Gardener.

I use the word "professional" guardedly. Somewhere in this land he must still survive, the gnarled, wise old man who has forgotten more about what goes on in the earth than Max Schling ever knew. I have never met one, however, outside an English novel. When we began here we could scarcely hire even a pair of willing hands and a strong back. What we got (when we absolutely had to have help with excavating and bulldozing and purchasing shrubs) were super-salesmen, eager to sell us rhododendron without roots, mulch that burned the grass, and contracts more costly than a yacht. They weeded not, neither did they thin. They all answered to the name of Mario, but if they were Italian they must have emigrated from concrete cities. Like Greeks who become restaurant keepers by propinquity, like Chinese who invariably set up laundries, these were innocent of apprenticeship in their trade. They pulled ferns instead of ragweed and planted bulbs upside down. They did not, at least, do to us what they did to friends of ours. These innocents owned two impressive evergreen trees which began to look very ill in the autumn. Their needles fell, their green dimmed. "Dead," announced the Professional Gardener. "I'll cut 'em down cheap." So he cut down the two finest larch trees in the village, which had *always* shed their needles in the fall like proper larches. Still, at twelve dollars a day (I hear it is now twenty) they managed more damage from time to time than a siege of tent caterpillars. One summer when we had to be away on business, we left a highly recommended fellow to mow and weed. I also left him instructions about the lobelia—three hundred of them—which I had painstakingly planted for edging all around the front border. If anyone has ever planted three hundred lobelia the size of paperclips and much less sturdy, he will know my grief when we returned to find that purple edging looking like a patient who has just had drawn every other tooth in his head. It's been a long time now since we let any hands but ours touch lawn or garden. Power mowers and perseverance have saved us from one enemy.

But how can a gardener escape the burdens of his own toil? As I said before, it's success that makes him old before his time.

The trouble with flowers is that they flower, with vegetables that they mature, and in spite of adversaries.

Already, although it is only May, the gardener's heady pleasure in creation is giving way to post-natal care. Narcissus has spent itself. Now he must trudge daily about the borders, snipping off those wizened heads. Hyacinths have to be propped up. Shortly it will be time to divide the iris, pinch off the rosebuds, examine the peony for spot, lift the early bulbs. Tulips must rest although he does not. Flower beds must be made smooth while his own is unslept in. For me especially, this year, how glorious not to have to think of pansies! For no one who grows them—and everyone does—is ever finished with them. Give a pansy an inch, and it takes a yard. On a place like ours, part sun, part shade, they used to emerge by the hundred like celebrities at a Rogers and Hammerstein first night. Every time I came out of doors I used to shudder at the sight of all those sulky, staring little faces. I felt as if I had no privacy. Besides, they had to be picked so they wouldn't run to seed and make *more* pansies. And what do you do with them after you have picked a daily fistful? Give them to friends? All your friends are having pansy trouble too. There are just so many vases which will hold their stubby stems, just so many low bowls which can be filled. They are worse than petunias, which, although I soon eliminated them as garden *décor*, I always rather admired. Petunias are so valiant! They will grow anywhere—on the seashore, in window boxes, in poor soil or wealthy. They are as hard to kill and as perky as slum children; and when every other edging fails, petunias can be bought as seedlings at a fairly moderate price.

But for poppies I have no use at all. If they are hybrids, they die out in a year or two. If they are ordinary ones, their only possible virtue is to fill in that color gap between tulips and roses. Then they spread like measles in a prep school. I used to find poppies crowding out the cape marigold, three beds away. They infest the hemerocallis, intrude on the nemophila, pop up in cutting beds and on the lawn. I learned to pull them with the same ruthlessness I used on bindweed.

As a matter of fact, one grows weary of all the hardy bloomers, of everything which has to be reaped and gathered. By July, keeping flowers in the house gets too much for the working gardener. Early bouquets are valuable for morale, and they endure. But by midsummer, worn out with carrying water to his seedlings, with ashing the delphinium, putting pots over transplants, and worrying about flea-beetle on the polyanthus, he gets a little desperate trying to use up all that blossoming. He can't be making Williamsburg arrangements and pruning the hedge too.

(While I am about it, let me mention the facts of life concerning pruning. It should always be done by women. Men can't be trusted with pruning shears any more than they can be trusted with the grocery money in a delicatessen. Something comes over a man when he has that weapon in his hands. Drunk with power, he destroys lilac bushes, reduces the taxus to a shred, and cuts back the euonymous until it will not leaf again for two seasons. They are like boys with new pocket knives who will not stop whittling. I got so that I used to follow my husband around with a little bell to ring when the blood-lust of cutting took possession of him.)

But if flowers become a burden, how much more wearing is a harvest of vegetables! Again, wealth can be dismaying. You can let campanula just stand and look handsome. But peas have to be eaten. Cabbages must be gathered. The successful truck gardener can never go out to dinner in the summer or spend a week end away, because his conscience tells him he has to be at home eating up his corn or packaging his beans for the freezer. Vegetables were the first thing we let go, and thankfully. For a while

we planted tomatoes in the flower border, and once we
made a handsome edging out of lettuces. But the tomatoes
drooped upon the zinnias in August, and when we picked
a lettuce it destroyed the symmetry of our beds. Now we
just buy what we need at the grocer's.

You must not mistake me. I have spoken of the burdens
of success, but as many gardens are sprinkled with tears as
with lime sulphate. We too have had our failures. Delphinium we nursed season after season yet could not make
it settle down successfully for more than two years. Our
lupin ate the ground away from its neighbors. We were
hopeless with certain strains of chrysanthemum. As for
my favorite of all flowers, sweet peas, we found that what
the experts told us was correct—they will not grow in the
climate of Westchester County. With a stubborn belief in
miracles, I planted them for several springs anyhow, each
year a little earlier and more scientifically. But with the
first June heat wave my poor vines scorched on their
strings as if a fire had withered them.

Disappointments, though, only whet the gardener's zeal.
Every time we failed we bit our lips and tried something
else. If sweet peas refused to climb, our roses did not. If
we were unsuccessful with the gaudy fire-thorn, we could
improve our clematis. For each failure there was some
triumph. Even our inability to raise nasturtiums did not
cast us down. Those cheerful flowers, which every farm-
wife can grow, were as bad as the sweet peas. Sickly and
sparse, they so welcomed the black-bean aphid that we were
in despair until I found the right note in our gardening

book. "Nasturtiums," I read, "thrive best in a poor soil." We comforted ourselves with the thought of our pernicious riches.

For early on in our obsession my husband had become a compost-heap enthusiast, and we started enriching our half-acre like crazy.

The compost heap probably deserves a chapter to itself. "Compost" says the dictionary, "is a term applied to any loose, friable soil-preparation resulting from the laying of alternate layers of fresh manure and any suitable absorbent material. Added to the soil, it supplies both humus and plant-food in safe, convenient form."

So much for definitions. In reality the compost pile is the gardener's Holy Grail, his end rather than his means, the outward and visible sign of his inward dedication. Ours we established at the bottom of a shady bit of lawn under a mulberry tree. Into it went everything remotely like humus—grass clippings, excess of seedlings, leaves, cans of old bacon grease, expensive manure, phosphates, and love. Turning it over, touching it to see if it was warm, straining it, just standing there and watching it ferment, took so much of my husband's time for a while that it was all I could do to get him to attach the sprinkler system. The heap grew slowly, but it grew steadily and it fermented. And one day we had what we had been waiting for—worms! The right kind of worms is what the gardener boasts about.

I remember one summer day when friends of ours drove over from New Jersey for dinner, and before they had the car door open the sportive flower-grower in the front seat was brandishing a basket of soil and shouting, "Look! I've got worms too!"

Compost people are evangelists. Once when the mission was fresh upon us we took a short trip through New England (it must have been between seasons), visiting friends in country houses on the way. In our wake, like an excursion steamer, we left a trail of debris, little piles of humus and clippings guaranteed to do wonders, my dears, for the garden next year or the year after. Gentlemen who hadn't handled a spade in a generation found themselves out in the back field turning over manure, when all they wanted to do was settle down on the terrace with a martini. We must have been the guests whose parting was *really* speeded.

That compost is good for the soil is undeniable. That the heap itself is an eyesore unless one has several acres of ground is also true; and no matter how hard we tried to disguise ours with vines and leafy overhang, it scarred the property. In fact, it still does; for that is the last thing which we are eliminating. Still, little by little we shovel it onto the shrubbery, and some day there will be nothing left but an empty wooden box which we can break up for the fire.

I can't recall exactly which day and hour it was that we decided we must reform, when my husband and I stared round our grounds and with a wild surmise came to a decision. It may have been the time he was recovering from a slipped disk sustained from having lifted one too many spadefuls of mulch. It may have been that day at lunch when we suddenly agreed that we didn't like radishes and why were we raising them—just because they were a foolproof crop? Or perhaps it was the hot afternoon I rebelled at having to clip off one more flower to keep the buddleia in health. We had probably also been poking into the garage, where were stored all the costly tools of our avocation—all the patented weeders and all the pots and frames and hose-racks and bags of lime which we had accumulated. Maybe it was too many pansies. For one fateful moment we looked back over eighteen years and decided a garden wasn't worth it.

We hadn't been abroad since we bought the house. I hadn't ever felt solvent enough to acquire a mink coat, or my husband to buy a decent chess set. Yes, we did have flowers too many to pick and apples we could have bought cheaper in any store (what with delayed dormant sprays, pink bud sprays, petal-fall or calyx spray, and the other four or five expensive protections). We had the finest Madonna lilies in the village, but we couldn't leave for even a summer Sunday lest blight or drought or roving animal disturb the peace. Even the winters were not our own, for our mania had pushed us into cellar-forcing, and all through February we drowned in a sea of hyacinths and early fringed tulips. (I used to rejoice when my friends had to have operations. I then had a legitimate excuse to share the wealth.) We had cultivated the arbutus and the lady-slipper in our wild border, but we were in danger of letting our minds run to seed. We knew how to grow gypsophilia to add to bouquets of Betty Prior Floribunda roses, but we hadn't yet seen *My Fair Lady*.

It was time we dispossessed ourselves.

I think I never knew the feel of freedom better than the glorious morning I gave away all the young digitalis plants I had been nurturing in a semi-shaded spot; unless it was when I heard the lawn-mower scrunch over the carcass of an obstinate phlox. For our blueprint of destruction was simple. We returned the land to greenery, just as we had found it when we came. Every border went into ivy or periwinkle. Under trees we planted ajuga. The flower beds became lawn. As for pachysandra, that we strewed like manna. I feel for the anonymous genius who first discovered that useful ground cover the same sort of gratitude that parents feel for Dr. Jonas Salk. Pachysandra has been our summer immunizer. You can't kill it, it grows faster than sedum, no weeds live in it, and it stays green all winter. It even hides the ragged edges of the lawn and needs no more cultivation than its own mulch and a nice acid soil. We've left the hedges—after all, a man has to have *some* exercise—and we've left the roses so long as they climb up trellises where they behave themselves and don't require more than a little careless clipping. Besides, climbers deserve to be saved. A Paul Scarlet for two dollars from the nearest nursery gives more for its money than even a flat of petunias, and that is giant praise. We've even left the tulips and daffodils and azaleas and whatever forget-me-nots survive the winters. A bit of spring color revives us, and we've put enough fern and pachysandra near them to defend us against weeds. Everything else is neat, green, and undemanding. We can go away any time we like and, except for the encroachments of crab grass, all will be tidy when we return.

It is true that, like alcoholics, we shall never be truly cured. I scarcely dare keep violas on a southern window sill lest they prove the opening wedge of a new indoor-gardening mania. We never pass a border in full bloom that we do not feel a pang of envy—envy mixed with gratitude that it is not ours to spray and weed. When I give a party—and I do give them, now that I have time—it is sometimes awkward to have no bloom of our own for the table.

But by and large we are content with our roles as elder statesmen to whom our toiling younger neighbors can come for advice and praise. And we don't really miss a harvest. In the summer we do our friends the favor of accepting their flowers, and in the fall we gladden their hearts by eating up their tomatoes. It's a nice change all around. They know the joy of giving, we of receiving. And since I have all those low bowls left over in the china closet, I'm a godsend to every woman in the block.

I pick their pansies for them.

# Some of My Best Friends . . .

Aᴌᴛʜᴏᴜɢʜ the story goes that woman was contrived from Adam's rib, I have a different theory. In her public sense, she sprang full-panoplied out of his imagination. For centuries woman battened on male illusion, finding she was cherished in direct proportion to how well she lived up to her myth. Even today, with medicine and sociology chipping away at our legend so that we are in danger of losing much of our armor and a good deal of allure, certain misconceptions linger. We find it useful to foster them. So I hope I won't be read out of the party if I smash one more masculine belief—the belief that women dislike other women.

For quite the contrary is true. Women like other women fine. The more feminine she is, the more comfortable a woman feels with her own sex. It is only the occasional and therefore noticeable adventuress who refuses to make friends with us. (I speak now of genuine friendship. Our love we reserve for its proper object, man.)

What has been misconstrued, perhaps, is woman's behavior during what I must bluntly call the hunting season.

We are immensely practical. If the race is to continue, we like to provide a second parent. So we go about the serious business of finding husbands in a serious manner which allows no time for small luxuries like mercy toward competitors. Nature turns red in tooth and claw, every method is fair, and rivals get no quarter.

Once triumphant, however, with a man for our hearth, a fresh generation on its way, we sheathe our swords. We lay aside, as it were, certain secret weapons, and reaccept the company of our own kind. We choose each other for neighbors. We dress for one another's approval. We borrow loaves of bread, exchange recipes and sympathy, talk over our problems together. Watch women at cocktail parties. All eyes and smiles for the gentlemen at first, the safe (by which I mean the satisfactorily married) ladies begin gradually to drift away from the bantering males. They do it tactfully. The fiction must be maintained that men are their sole concern. But by almost imperceptible degrees women edge toward some sofa where another woman is ensconced. There, while the talk seethes and bubbles around them, they whisper cozily together of truly important things like baby-sitters and little dressmakers.

Do I imply by this that women are as frivolous and unintellectual as they have been accused of being in other eras? Or that the larger issues do not concern them? Far from it. I am simply trying to convey the natural attraction that binds us together. Those two women on the sofa might well go on from household problems to the lesser topics of literature, space rockets, or politics. I know. For I am frequently one of the ladies on the sofa. In other words, I like women.

My reasons are many and sufficient. I like them for their all-around, all-weather dependability. I like them because they are generally so steady, realistic, and careful about tidying up after a hot shower. I admire them for their prudence, thrift, gallantry, common sense, and knobless knees, and because they are neither so vain nor so given to emotion as their opposite numbers. I like the way they answer letters promptly, put shoe trees in their shoes at night, and are so durable physically. Their natures may not be so fine or their hearts so readily touched as man's, but they are not so easily imposed on either. I respect them, too, because they are so good at handling automobiles.

Don't misunderstand me. Some of my best friends are male drivers. And they seldom go to sleep at the wheel or drive 90 on a 45-mile-an-hour highway or commit any other of the sins of which statistics accuse them. But insurance companies have been busy as bees proving that I don't get around among the right people.

In New York State, where I live, they have even made it expensive to have sons. Car insurance costs twice as much if there are men in the family under twenty-five as if there are only women. Obviously the female of the species makes the best chauffeur. And well she ought. Women get the most practice. Aside from truck- and taxi-drivers, it is they who most consistently handle the cars of the nation. For five days of the week they are in command—slipping cleverly through the traffic on their thousand errands, park-

ing neatly in front of chain stores, ferrying their husbands
to and from commuting trains, driving the young to schools
and dentists and dancing classes and Scout meetings. It is
only on Saturdays and Sundays that men get their innings,
not to speak of their outings, and it is over week ends that
most of the catastrophes occur.

Not that I *blame* men. It is in their natures to dream
greatly, even amid traffic. The young ones cannot help
showing off to their dates, and the older ones must not be
held culpable for a tendency to compete with the red
Jaguar in front. It's just that I feel safer with a woman at
the wheel. For one thing, she is apt to get where she is
going with a minimum of fuss and temper. She is not too
proud to inquire directions, and when they are given to her
she listens. Men would rather pore endlessly over maps,
however inadequate, or else make out by intuition.

Now I have nothing against intuition. It is one of men's
inborn and most endearing qualities. But their trust in it
baffles the ordinary straight-thinking woman. In every field
from horse racing to national politics we prefer to marshal
facts, estimate them calmly, and then make our choices,
rather than rely on some sixth sense. Something is always
telling a man—some peculiar inner voice—that Senator
Humphrey Grough is really going to solve the farm problem, or that the storm windows don't need to go up this
week end because we're certain to have a mild November,
or that tonight is his lucky night and he's bound to fill that
inside straight.

There are, I admit, areas where intuition pays off. If

Columbus hadn't had a hunch that he could sail to India by way of the Atlantic Ocean, he'd never have bumped into San Salvador. Wellington felt in his bones that he could stop Napoleon at Waterloo, just as those prospectors in California felt there was gold lying around the vicinity; and their bones were speaking true. Moreover, few businesses could burgeon or stock markets flourish or plays get produced without the impulsiveness of Adam's heir.

Just the same, women choose to proceed less rashly. They know that if their hunches go astray they will have to pick up the pieces. Even in small things a woman likes to be guided by fact. Let her loose in a delicatessen and she comes out with the loaf of rye bread and the half-pint of cream which she had put down on her list instead of the olives stuffed with anchovies, the assorted cheeses, pumpernickels, pickles, herring, potato salad, breast of turkey, pastes, spreads, and relishes which her husband dreamed the larder might need over the week end. And if she has a sore throat she does not ignore it completely on the theory that rude germs go away if one doesn't speak to them, or else take, groaning, to her bed because she has an intuition she will die before nightfall. She consults her doctor or a thermometer.

Of course women can keep calm about illnesses because, as a sex, we are so much less fragile than men—a point which scarcely needs belaboring. Again, statistics prove it. Wives consistently outlive their husbands. If one of a pair of twins succumbs in infancy, it is nearly always the delicate boy rather than the sturdy girl. Despite the severer tensions of a woman's life (and what hard-driven executive would exchange his routine for the soul-lacerating vexations of a housewife's day?) we are not so prone to ulcers, alcoholism, or gout. We survive shipwreck, bankruptcy, and childbirth with notorious aplomb.

Even the small ordeals find us less vulnerable. We are brave at the dentist's, self-possessed in the doctor's office, and disinclined to faint while being vaccinated. Again, we deserve no credit. Providence simply has provided us with that extra bit of stamina.

Providence has, indeed, almost made men expendable—or is trying to. I read with apprehension last spring that scientists had found they could raise turkeys from unfertilized eggs without benefit of a male turkey. They called it parthenogenesis. The scientists when last heard from were dubiously experimenting with some of the higher vertebrates such as rabbits. It gives one to think.

Extra stamina accounts for much. It explains why, no matter how they may clamor for equality, men can never hope to compete with women in certain sports and occupations. Men may do well enough in less demanding fields. They can throw a ball overhand, hurl a discus about, climb an unimportant mountain. But put them down in a crowded department store at holiday time for some jolly scrimmage and they collapse at the first counter. A woman in three-inch heels, with a tote bag weighing forty pounds on her arm as handicap, can outwalk a man on a shopping expedition any day—and outdance him again at night. In

one morning she can wash, iron, turn mattresses, wrestle
with the sweeper, paper the ceiling of the dinette, and do
it on black coffee and a slice of toast.

Which brings me to another admirable female trait: the
ability to get along on a restricted diet. A husband before
breakfast is more terrible than an army with banners. De-
prive him of his lunch and he wilts like a plucked dandelion. And the dinnerless male is something too dismal to
contemplate. So, when undertaking a vital mission, women
like to have women for companions. They are not always
having to be stoked with food. If they *must* stop along the
line of march for sustenance, they are willing to settle for a
teashop instead of the most expensive café in town, and to
divide the bill fairly afterward. This I find consoling. One
of man's most exasperating qualities is his insistence on
lavish gestures when he is settling a restaurant charge.

Notice what happens when two couples are dining out.
Mr. and Mrs. Whitehouse, an unextravagant pair, have
taken the $3.50 blue-plate special with a martini apiece.
Mr. and Mrs. Blair have each downed two or three cocktails and gone on to beef tenderloin, asparagus hollandaise,
and for dessert something flaming in a silver dish. But
when the bill is brought, Mr. Whitehouse says expansively,
"We'll just split it," and pays his unequal share without a
murmur.

You won't catch us ladies behaving so. When we lunch
or dine together we tot up every item ("Marge, you had
the chicken sandwich on nut-and-raisin bread, and Evelyn,

did you order two cups of coffee with that lemon sponge?"), figure how the cost should fall, and even divide the tip in proper ratio.

It's this no-nonsense side of women that is pleasant to deal with. They are the real sportsmen. They don't constantly have to be building up frail egos by large public performances like overtipping the hat-check girl, speaking fluent French to the Hungarian waiter, and sending back the wine to be recooled. They are neither too proud to carry packages nor too timid to ask a dilatory clerk for service.

What I enjoy, too, about my feminine friends is their downright honesty. Ask a woman if she likes your hairdo and she *tells* you. Make a small bet with her and she expects to be paid. And when she passes on a bit of scandal, she doesn't call it "shop talk," thus lending it a spurious moral air. Of course we women gossip on occasion. But our appetite for it is not as avid as a man's. It is in the boys' gyms, the college fraternity houses, the club locker rooms, the paneled offices of business that gossip reaches its luxuriant flower. More tidbits float around the corridors of one major advertising firm in an afternoon than Louella Parsons ever matched in a year's output. Commuting trains buzz with it. The professions grow fat on it. The fluffiest blonde of a private secretary locks more secrets in her chic head than the granite-jawed tycoon who employs her. Women, in fact, are the secret-keepers. Forced by biological circumstance to live a subtler life than their brothers, they have learned to hold their tongues. "Kiss and tell" is a male and not a female slogan. There is something about man's naïve character, something less than flintlike in his soul, which makes him a poor risk for a confidence.

That additional flint in a woman helps her, moreover, to keep her head. She is not always out on some rash adventure—leading a lost cause, buying shares in El Dorado, or lending money to a brave little widow with nine famishing and nonexistent children. If we have not man's compassion, we also lack his gullibility.

And then from the purely technical point of view, I do like women's mechanical handiness. They are so reassuringly clever about mending things—about fixing locks on doors and putting in new fuses and repairing leaky faucets and stopping windows from rattling.

Now and then a gifted man sets out to be his own plumber or carpenter or electrician. But did you ever watch him at his work? To begin with, he must first invest in an elaborate set of tools, expensive as Russian sable. These he brings out lovingly, one by one, fondling them as a hunter does his rifles. Then he commandeers as helpers anyone unfortunate enough to be within earshot. People must hold things. Someone must hand him things. The ladder has to be supported. He has to have fetched to him, intermittently, sharpeners for his chisels, cloths for wiping his hands, hot water from the sink, and cups of coffee or cold drinks at frequent intervals. Papers must be laid down around him and the entire household listen to his exhortations, arguments, and complaints. Particularly, there must be some obliging menial to look on, admire, and deposit the laurel wreath on his brow when the job, as it sometimes does, gets finished. But I've seen women merely give a sharp slap to a reluctant washing machine or a dig in the ribs to a sulky toaster, and off it goes.

Mechanically deft as they are, not to speak of honest, clean, courteous, brave, reverent, and loyal, women are the proper objects of woman's admiration. Oh, why, I often wonder, in defiance of Henry Higgins, can't men be more like us!

But I always hear myself answering, "How splendid that they aren't!" Expendable they may be. But into our hard, practical lives they bring tenderness and sentiment. They give existence its meaning, its essential *élan*. They encourage our better natures. And they are esthetically so appealing too! Who better graces a drawing room? What prettier sight can one see at evening under the soft glow of the lamp than a man dressed in his old tweed jacket and lounging slippers?

No, without men we should be the poorer. Brightness would fall from the air, life would lose most of its color and all of its romance. And there would be no one to help us lift our monotonous daily burdens. Besides having to go to the office every morning, we would also have to write all the novels, paint all the pictures, start all the wars; and we have better business than that already. Women are the fulfilled sex. Through our children we are able to produce our own immortality, so we lack that divine restlessness which sends men charging off in pursuit of fortune or fame or an imagined Utopia. That is why we number so few geniuses among us. The wholesome oyster wears no pearl, the healthy whale no ambergris, and as long as we can keep on adding to the race, we harbor a sort of health within ourselves.

Sometimes I have a notion that what might improve the situation is to have women take over the occupations of government and trade and to give men their freedom. Let them do what they are best at. While we scrawl interoffice memos and direct national or extranational affairs, men could spend *all* their time inventing wheels, peering at stars, composing poems, carving statues, exploring continents—discovering, reforming, or crying out in a sacramental wilderness. Efficiency would probably increase, and no one would have to worry so much about the Gaza Strip or an election.

On the other hand, though, I like our status too much to make the suggestion seriously. For everybody knows it's a man's world and they have not managed it very well, but at least it's theirs. If women took over, we might find ourselves thrashing around in the very masculine morasses we have so far managed to avoid.

# I Knew Mrs. Tuttle

IT MUST be that I lack a certain inner warmth possessed and exploited by my more spectacular friends. This refulgence of the spirit is always leading them into little adventures, wittier and more human than mine. The strangest people confide in them. They are continually encountering a taxi-driver who reads Proust, a kindly and humorous laundress, a man who runs a newsstand and knew John Reed. The boy who shines their shoes recites poetry of his own making, and their charwomen leave behind them misspelled notes amazing enough to make lovely dinner conversation. Somehow such characters elude me.

The shabby waiter who fetches my filet of sole may wear the lines of suffering in his patient face, but whether from nostalgia or bunions I will never learn. The utmost information I can pry out of him concerns the fact that there's no more spumoni today and he doesn't know about the apple cake. My cleaning woman spells somewhat more confidently than I, and anyhow her *billets-doux* are mere lists like, "Please order: 1 chamois, 1 bottle ammonia."

Yet when I fall to brooding on this lack in me, this inability to discover the quaint and the unusual in the passing throng, I comfort myself with one reflection. After all, I knew Mrs. Tuttle.

Yes, I knew Mrs. Tuttle, and she was mine. Others were acquainted with her, could break her bread or pass the time of day; but it was in my presence alone that Mrs. Tuttle's extraordinary genius had its finest blooming.

Not that Mrs. Tuttle falls into any of the categories I have mentioned. On the contrary, Mrs. T. was landed gentry, the comfortable widow of a former feed-store proprietor in the Connecticut town where my husband and I once spent a summer. A placid and ample lady of late middle age, she owned a solid reputation in the village as a good if somewhat tight-fisted housekeeper, a member of the Ladies' Aid, a taxpayer. The village praised her spice cake annually at the Baked Bean Supper. So far as I know, her soul was untroubled by literary yearnings, and she had traveled extensively only between our village and West Hartford, where one of her daughters lived, happily married to a veterinarian. Yet great were her talents.

The square white house we rented that season stood across a shady lane from hers, and I used to see her moving, stately among the foxgloves in her small garden. At first we would nod amiably as we passed, but it was some time before our acquaintance took on a friendlier aspect. Then one lucky afternoon I ran across the lane to implore the use of her telephone. Ours was out of order. Mrs. Tuttle, coming to the door in a worn dressing gown, her hair clustered with bobby pins, graciously put me at my ease.

"You must excuse my appearance," she said with dignified politeness. "I have just been decomposing." And, very *de rigueur mortis,* she led me to the phone.

"You made it up," my husband accused me that night at dinner. "People simply don't say such things."

We passed it off, finally, as the solitary lapse of a confused elderly lady. I was to find, however, that Mrs. Tuttle could toss off such gems with the dexterity of a Chesterton composing paradoxes. Provided, that is, I was the audience.

For Mrs. Tuttle was a Malaprop of the first water, an inspired word-mangler, a lady in whom Dickens would have rejoiced. And the remarkable thing is that, during the months of our stay in the town, she improvised her enthralling sentences for my ears alone. My husband repeatedly egged her on. Nothing happened.

She called on me quite formally the following week, carrying an old-fashioned parasol and wearing a good deal of coral jewelry. I sat on the sofa, regaled her with tea and nut bread, and listened to her ponderous comments on the weather and the difficulty of getting real good service at the grocery store. It was as the talk veered to Mrs. Tuttle's contemplated visit to her daughter in West Hartford that she reared back and passed another miracle.

"I'm combining business with pleasure," she announced primly. "I plan to see the eye-noculist while I'm there."

The teacup wavered in my hand, but she swept on grandly.

"I've broken the glands of my spectacles," she said, "and

I can't get them rightly repaired here. So I'm going to take them to the Hartford man—costive as he is."

Monday I ran across her at the post office and offered to drive her home. She accepted with pleasure, volunteering that her ancient Ford "cupolo" was languishing in the village garage and no knowing when it would be running again, with the worthless help Mr. Hatfield employed in the place. Once when the radiator had leaked, she told me, he had kept her waiting three weeks.

"But this time," said Mrs. Tuttle, "I've told him he must have it done by Thursday, or he loses my business. I simply laid down my automaton."

My spouse grunted skeptically when he heard this. I could see the envy consuming his soul.

There was the time she beckoned me and asked me to come over to see her dining-room table, set for a Ladies' Aid meeting.

"I'm serving bologna sandwiches," she told me, "with men's dressing." And she went on to assure me that she was "diabolically opposed" to the view held by Mrs. Whitmark that the group members always should provide a three-course luncheon.

Once we walked down the lane together, pursued by a small black terrier, which yipped at our heels and shook even Mrs. Tuttle's monumental calm. At last she stopped and lifted her parasol threateningly.

"If that dog," she exclaimed, "doesn't stop following me, he'll simply have to suffer the contents!"

The tranquil summer passed. The leaf fell, the maple blazed, the cordwood piled high in village sheds. One of Mrs. Tuttle's grandchildren spent a week with her and acquired as a pet a spirited white rabbit, which Mrs. T. described tolerantly to me as a cunning thing that "can do all sorts of tricks. You ought to see it jump through a person's arms and beg for carrots. Why, it's a regular maniac!" We supplied "acrobat," perhaps incorrectly.

Our neighbor was sorry to see us go back to town, she said. She would miss us, particularly my husband. "You have a fine man," she assured me privately not long before we left, "such a redundance of good humor."

I agreed, for his optimism *is* at times a little overwhelming.

We promised that we would be back if we could, though perhaps not next season, since we were planning to make a trip to California by way of the Panama Canal.

Mrs. Tuttle pricked up her ears. "You won't like Panama," she warned me. "One of my nieces is married and living there, and she says the heat is something terrible."

"We won't be there long enough to mind," I reassured her vaguely, "although I expect it *is* a pretty warm place. It's only nine degrees above the equator, you know."

Mrs. Tuttle seemed surprised by this piece of information. She pondered, and then, as though she were providing me with a farewell token, she scaled new heights of language. "I hadn't realized that," she commented brightly. "Nine degrees above the equator, you say. All the year around?"

# From My Terrace

# Suburbia, of Thee I Sing

TWENTY miles east of New York City as the New Haven Railroad flies sits a village I shall call Spruce Manor. The Boston Post Road, there, for the length of two blocks, becomes Main Street, and on one side of that thundering thoroughfare are the grocery stores and the drug stores and the Village Spa where teen-agers gather of an afternoon to drink their Cokes and speak their curious confidences. There one finds the shoe repairers and the dry cleaners and the second-hand stores which sell "antiques," and the stationery stores which dispense comic books to ten-year-olds and greeting cards and lending-library masterpieces to their mothers. On the opposite side stand the bank, the fire house, the public library. The rest of this town of perhaps five or six thousand people lies to the south and is bounded largely by Long Island Sound, curving protectively on three borders. The movie theater (dedicated to the showing of second-run, single-feature pictures) and the grade schools lie north, beyond the Post Road, and that is a source of worry to Spruce Manorites. They are always a little uneasy about the children, crossing, perhaps, before the lights are safely green. However, two excellent policemen—Mr. Crowley and Mr. Lang—station themselves at the intersections four times a day, and so far there have been no accidents.

Spruce Manor in the spring and summer and fall is a pretty town, full of gardens and old elms. (There are few spruces but the village council is considering planting some on the station plaza, out of sheer patriotism.) In the winter, the houses reveal themselves as comfortable, well kept, architecturally insignificant. Then one can see the town for what it is and has been since it left off being farm and woodland some sixty years ago—the epitome of Suburbia, not the country and certainly not the city. It is a commuter's town, the living center of a web which unrolls each morning as the men swing aboard the locals, and contracts again in the evening when they return. By day, with even the children pent in schools, it is a village of women. They trundle mobile baskets at the A & P, they sit under driers at the hairdressers, they sweep their porches and set out bulbs and stitch up slipcovers. Only on week ends does it become heterogeneous and lively, the parking places difficult to find.

Spruce Manor has no country club of its own, though devoted golfers have their choice of two or three not far away. It does have a small yacht club and a beach which can be used by anyone who rents or owns a house here. The village supports a little park with playground equipment and a counselor, where children, unattended by parents, can spend summer days if they have no more pressing engagements.

It is a town not wholly without traditions. Residents will point out the two-hundred-year-old Manor house, now a minor museum; and in the autumn they line the streets on a scheduled evening to watch the volunteer firemen parade. That is a fine occasion, with so many heads of households marching in their red blouses and white gloves, some with flaming helmets, some swinging lanterns, most of them genially out of step. There is a bigger parade on Memorial Day, with more marchers than watchers and with the Catholic priest, the rabbi, and the Protestant ministers each delivering a short prayer when the paraders gather near the war memorial. On the whole, however, outside of contributing generously to the Community Chest, Manorites are not addicted to municipal get-togethers.

No one is very poor here and not many families rich enough to be awesome. In fact, there is not much to distinguish Spruce Manor from any other of a thousand suburbs outside of New York City or San Francisco or Detroit or Chicago or even Stockholm, for that matter. Except for one thing. For some reason, Spruce Manor has become a sort of symbol to writers and reporters familiar only with its name or trivial aspects. It has become a symbol of all that is middle-class in the worst sense, of settled-downness or rootlessness, according to what the writer is trying to prove; of smug and prosperous mediocrity—or even, in more lurid novels, of lechery at the country club and Sunday-morning hangovers.

To condemn Suburbia has long been a literary cliché, anyhow. I have yet to read a book in which the suburban life was pictured as the good life or the commuter as a sympathetic figure. He is nearly as much a stock character as the old stage Irishman: the man who "spends his life riding to and from his wife," the eternal Babbitt who knows all about Buicks and nothing about Picasso, whose sanctuary is the club locker room, whose ideas spring ready-made from the illiberal newspapers. His wife plays politics at the P.T.A. and keeps up with the Joneses. Or—if the scene is more gilded and less respectable—the commuter is the high-powered advertising executive with a station wagon and an eye for the ladies, his wife a restless baggage given to too many cocktails in the afternoon.

These clichés I challenge. I have lived in the country. I have lived in the city. I have lived in an average Middle Western small town. But for the best fifteen years of my life I have lived in Suburbia, and I like it.

"Compromise!" cried our friends when we came here from an expensive, inconvenient, moderately fashionable tenement in Manhattan. It was the period in our lives when everyone was moving somewhere—farther uptown, farther downtown, across town to Sutton Place, to a half-dozen rural acres in Connecticut or New Jersey or even Vermont. But no one in our rather rarefied little group was thinking of moving to the suburbs except us. They were aghast that we could find anything appealing in the thought of a middle-class house on a middle-class street in a middle-class village full of middle-class people. That we were tired of town and hoped for children, that we couldn't afford both a city apartment and a farm, they put down as feeble excuses. To this day they cannot understand us. You see, they read the books. They even write them.

Compromise? Of course we compromise. But compromise, if not the spice of life, is its solidity. It is what makes nations great and marriages happy and Spruce Manor the pleasant place it is. As for its being middle-class, what is wrong with acknowledging one's roots? And how free we are! Free of the city's noise, of its ubiquitous doormen, of the soot on the window sill and the radio in the next apartment. We have released ourselves from the seasonal hegira to the mountains or the seashore. We have only one address, one house to keep supplied with paring knives and blankets. We are free from the snows that block the countryman's roads in winter and his electricity which always goes off in a thunderstorm. I do not insist that we are typical. There is nothing really typical about any of our friends and neighbors here, and therein lies my point. The true suburbanite needs to conform less than anyone else; much less than the gentleman farmer with his remodeled salt-box or than the determined cliff-dweller with his necessity for living at the right address. In Spruce Manor all addresses are right. And since we are fairly numerous here, we need not fall back on the people nearest of us for total companionship. There is not here, as in a small city away from truly urban centers, some particular family whose codes must be ours. And we could not keep up with the Joneses even if we wanted to, for we know many

Joneses and they are all quite different people leading the most various lives.

The Albert Joneses spend their week ends sailing, the Bertram Joneses cultivate their delphinium, the Clarence Joneses—Clarence being a handy man with a cello—are enthusiastic about amateur chamber music. The David Joneses dote on bridge, but neither of the Ernest Joneses understands it and they prefer staying home of an evening so that Ernest Jones can carve his witty caricatures out of pieces of old fruit wood. We admire one another's gardens, applaud one another's sailing records; we are too busy to compete. So long as our clapboards are painted and our hedges decently trimmed, we have fulfilled our community obligations. We can live as anonymously as in a city or we can call half the village by their first names.

On our half-acre or three-quarters, we can raise enough tomatoes for our salads and assassinate enough beetles to satisfy the gardening urge. Or we can buy our vegetables at the store and put the whole place to lawn without feeling that we are neglecting our property. We can have privacy and shade and the changing of the seasons and also the Joneses next door from whom to borrow a cup of sugar or a stepladder. Despite the novelists, the shadow of the country club rests lightly on us. Half of us wouldn't be found dead with a golf stick in our hands, and loathe Saturday dances. Few of us expect to be deliriously wealthy or world-famous or divorced. What we do expect is to pay off the mortgage and send our healthy children to good colleges.

For when I refer to life here, I think, of course, of living with children. Spruce Manor without children would be a paradox. The summer waters are full of them, gamboling like dolphins. The lanes are alive with them, the yards overflow with them, they possess the tennis courts and the skating pond and the vacant lots. Their roller skates wear down the asphalt and their bicycles make necessary the twenty-five-mile speed limit. They converse interminably on the telephones and make rich the dentist and the pediatrician. Who claims that a child and a half is the American middle-class average? A nice medium Spruce Manor family runs to four or five, and we count proudly, but not with amazement, the many solid households running to six, seven, eight, nine, even up to twelve. Our houses here are big and not new, most of them, and there is a temptation to fill them up, let the *décor* fall where it may.

Besides, Spruce Manor seems designed by Providence and town planning for the happiness of children. Better designed than the city; better, I say defiantly, than the country. Country mothers must be constantly arranging and contriving for their children's leisure time. There is no neighbor child next door for playmate, no school within walking distance. The ponds are dangerous to young swimmers, the woods full of poison ivy, the romantic dirt roads unsuitable for bicycles. An extra acre or two gives a fine sense of possession to an adult; it does not compensate children for the give-and-take of our village, where there is always a contemporary to help swing the skipping rope or put on the catcher's mitt. Where in the country is the

Friday-evening dancing class or the Saturday-morning movie (approved by the P.T.A.)? It is the greatest fallacy of all time that children love the country as a year-around plan. Children would take a dusty corner of Washington Square or a city sidewalk, even, in preference to the lonely sermons in stones and books in running brooks which their contemporaries cannot share.

As for the horrors of bringing up progeny in the city, for all its museums and other cultural advantages (so perfectly within reach of suburban families if they feel strongly about it), they were summed up for me one day last winter. The harried mother of one, speaking to me on the telephone just after Christmas, sighed and said, "It's been a really wonderful time for me, as vacations go. Barbara has had an engagement with a child in our apartment house every afternoon this week. I have had to take her almost nowhere." Barbara is eleven. For six of those eleven years, I realized, her mother must have dreaded Christmas vacation, not to mention spring, as a time when Barbara had to be entertained. I thought thankfully of my own daughters, whom I had scarcely seen since school closed, out with their skis and their sleds and their friends, sliding down the roped-off hill half a block away, coming in hungrily for lunch and disappearing again, hearty, amused, and safe —at least as safe as any sled-borne child can be.

Spruce Manor is not Eden, of course. Our taxes are higher than we like, and there is always that 8:02 in the morning to be caught, and we sometimes resent the necessity of rushing from a theater to a train on a weekday

evening. But the taxes pay for our really excellent schools
and for our garbage collections (so that the pails of orange
peels need not stand in the halls overnight as ours did in
the city) and for our water supply, which does not give
out every dry summer as it frequently does in the country.
As for the theaters—they are twenty miles away and we
don't get to them more than twice a month. But neither, I
think, do many of our friends in town. The 8:02 is rather
a pleasant train, too, say the husbands; it gets them to work
in thirty-four minutes, and they read the papers restfully
on the way.

"But the suburban mind!" cry our diehard friends in
Manhattan and Connecticut. "The suburban conversation!
The monotony!" They imply that they and I must scintil-
late or we perish. Let me anatomize Spruce Manor, for
them and for the others who envision Suburbia as a congregation of mindless housewives and amoral go-getters.

From my window, now, on a June morning, I have a
view. It contains neither solitary hills nor dramatic sky-
scrapers. But I can see my roses in bloom, and my foxglove,
and an arch of trees over the lane. I think comfortably of
my friends whose houses line this and other streets rather
like it. Not one of them is, so far as I know, doing any of
the things that suburban ladies are popularly supposed to
be doing. One of them, I happen to know, has gone bowl-
ing for her health and figure, but she has already tidied
up her house and arranged to be home before the boys return from school. Some, undoubtedly, are ferociously busy
in the garden. One lady is on her way to Ellis Island, bear-

ing comfort and gifts to a Polish boy—a seventeen-year-old stowaway who did slave labor in Germany and was liberated by a cousin of hers during the war—who is being held for attempting to attain the land of which her cousin told him. The boy has been on the island for three months. Twice a week she takes this tedious journey, meanwhile besieging courts and immigration authorities on his behalf. This lady has a large house, a part-time maid, and five children.

My friend around the corner is finishing her third novel. She writes daily from nine-thirty until two. After that her son comes back from school and she plunges into maternity; at six she combs her pretty hair, refreshes her lipstick, and is charming to her doctor husband. The village dancing school is run by another neighbor, as it has been for twenty years. She has sent a number of ballerinas on to the theatrical world as well as having shepherded for many a successful season the white-gloved little boys and full-skirted little girls through their first social tasks.

Some of the ladies are no doubt painting their kitchens or a nursery; one of them is painting the portrait, on assignment, of a very distinguished personage. Some of them are nurses' aides and Red Cross workers and supporters of good causes. But all find time to be friends with their families and to meet the 5:32 five nights a week. They read something besides the newest historical novel, Braque is not unidentifiable to most of them, and their conversation is for the most part as agreeable as the tables they set. The tireless bridge players, the gossips, the women bored by

their husbands live perhaps in our suburb, too. Let them.
Our orbits need not cross.

And what of the husbands, industriously selling bonds
or practicing law or editing magazines or looking through
microscopes or managing offices in the city? Do they spend
their evenings and their week ends in the gaudy bars of
52nd Street? Or are they the perennial householders, their
lives a dreary round of taking down screens and mending
drains? Well, screens they have always with them, and a
man who is good around the house can spend happy hours
with the plumbing even on a South Sea island. Some of
them cut their own lawns and some of them try to break
par and some of them sail their little boats all summer with
their families for crew. Some of them are village trustees
for nothing a year, and some listen to symphonies, and
some think Steve Allen ought to be President. There is a
scientist who plays wonderful bebop, and an insurance
salesman who has bought a big old house nearby and with
his own hands is gradually tearing it apart and reshaping
it nearer to his heart's desire. Some of them are passionate
hedge-clippers, and some read Plutarch for fun. But I do
not know many—though there may be such—who either
kiss their neighbors' wives behind doors or whose idea of
sprightly talk is to tell you the plot of an old movie.

It is June, now, as I have said. This afternoon my daughters will come home from school with a crowd of their
peers at their heels. They will eat up the cookies and drink
up the ginger ale and go down for a swim at the beach if
the water is warm enough, that beach which is only three

blocks away and open to all Spruce Manor. They will go unattended by me, since they have been swimming since they were four, and besides there are life guards and no big waves. (Even our piece of ocean is a compromise.) Presently it will be time for us to climb into our very old Studebaker—we are not car-proud in Spruce Manor—and meet the 5:32. That evening expedition is not vitally necessary, for a bus runs straight down our principal avenue from the station to the shore, and it meets all trains. But it is an event we enjoy. There is something delightfully ritualistic about the moment when the train pulls in and the men swing off, with the less sophisticated children running squealing to meet them. The women move over from the driver's seat, surrender the keys, and receive an absentminded kiss. It is the sort of picture that wakes John Marquand screaming from his sleep. But, deluded people that we are, we do not realize how mediocre it all seems. We will eat our undistinguished meal, probably without even a cocktail to enliven it. We will drink our coffee at the table, not carry it into the living room; if a husband changes for dinner here it is into old and spotty trousers and more comfortable shoes. The children will then go through the regular childhood routine—complain about their homework, grumble about going to bed, and finally accomplish both ordeals. Perhaps later the Gerard Joneses will drop in. We will talk a great deal of unimportant chatter and compare notes on food prices; we will also discuss the headlines and disagree. (Some of us in the Manor are Republicans, some are Democrats, a few lean plainly leftward. There are probably anti-Semites and anti-Catholics and even anti-Americans. Most of us are merely anti-antis.) We will all have one highball and the Joneses will leave early. Tomorrow and tomorrow and tomorrow the pattern will be repeated. This is Suburbia.

But I think that some day people will look back on our little interval here, on our Spruce Manor way of life, as we now look back on the Currier and Ives kind of living, with nostalgia and respect. In a world of terrible extremes, it will stand out as the safe, important medium.

Suburbia, of thee I sing!

# Purple Was for Danger

IN THE kingdom of childhood customs alter slowly. As I write this, in early June, the skipping-rope turns, the baseball thuds in the hand, exactly as they did when I was a citizen of that great nation.

"Strawberry *short*cake, cream on *tart*. Tell me the *name* of your sweet*heart*," chant two little girls, furiously whirling the rope in our back yard. And one by one the other little girls, their curls flying, their cheeks violently pink from exertion and joy, jump ecstatically, shouting the letters of the alphabet to J, for Johnnie, or to C, for Carter, or to whichever letter signifies the name of the reigning hero.

"Salt, vinegar, mustard, *pepper!*" they shriek, bobbing like corks on a wave. "Rinny Tin *Tin*," they shout, "swallowed a *pin*; went to the *doc*tor, but the *doc*tor wasn't in." The rope spins high as they gasp out the sad tiding. "He opened the *door*, fell on the *floor*, and that was the *end*"— now comes a quick confusion of hemp and skimming feet —"of Rinny Tin *Tin!*"

How many summers ago did I myself leap to the same tune, the same rhythms, except that we used a different name to rhyme with "in"? Nothing else has changed except the costumes. Down the street they are bouncing balls with a technique dazzling to adult eyes.

"A, my name is *Alice*," they sing, deftly putting the ball through its paces. "My *hus*band's name is *An*dy. He lives in *At*lanta, and *he* sells *ap*ples."

No wonder the technique is good. Balls have been dancing to an almost identical chant since—who knows?—Cromwell's, Charlemagne's, Alexander's time? The words vary a bit, but the song goes on. Even in the variations, what editors call a time lag is evident. Young moderns desert the newest television puppet to run outdoors, crying to the bouncing of a ball, "Teddy bear, Teddy bear, touch your dirty shoe. Teddy bear, Teddy bear, twenty-three, skiddoo!"

Even in my day, that slogan was past history, recalled by my mother in a reminiscent mood. A hundred years from now children may be singing it still as they "hop on one foot, hop on two," with no knowledge that they are commemorating an era.

Children are the true reactionaries, and the continuity of childhood is the peculiar solace of parenthood. In their play, we are immortal.

But though customs alter slowly, they do alter. What, for instance, has become of the wonderful game we used to play called Ante-I-Over, or simply Ante-Over? My children never heard of it. They drew the same designs for Hopscotch as we did. They graduated from Drop the Handkerchief, Huckle Buckle Beanstalk, and Hide-and-

Seek, to the grown-up Treasure Hunt. They sketched great circles in the snow and played Fox and Geese. They knew Cops and Robbers and Wolf and Blindman's Buff and Follow the Leader, and gave their forfeits when there came "an old lady with a stick and a staff" or a visitor from "New Orleens." But they never heard of Ante-I-Over.

We used some sort of soft ball, I remember, or, when that was not available and there were boys with strong arms on the team, a basketball. Our team threw it over some low building and then scattered; as soon as the other team caught it, they came running around the building to tag us. When we were all caught, we "chose up" again and changed sides. Then once more we threw it over—over what? Of course, over a barn! A nice low barn with plenty of space around it for the desperate challenge that followed the throwing. But there are no barns any more, even in our village. There are only garages, and most of them attached to houses. How can you run around an attached building? So there is one less delight.

The barns are gone; the back yards have grown smaller or have been turned into patios, complete with outdoor grills and redwood furniture. There is no place for Ante-I-Over. And where are the vacant lots? Those were our essential stamping grounds. There we chose up sides for Prisoner's Base and Pom-Pom Pullaway, for Crack the Whip, Fox and Hares, and something deliriously active called Kick the Can. In our village, tranquil with gardens and old elms, vacant lots are scarce. Or else they are protected from stampeding youngsters by signs that say "No Trespassing."

Basically, of course, the games go on. Do you remember Statue? The feminine contingent still plays that on summer afternoons. But it seems stodgier than I recall it. Do you remember Touch Wood and Cheeseit? They haven't changed—except that Cheeseit is now called Red Light, a purely modern flourish. And there is something called Giant Steps (this is for the younger set), which I would believe they had invented except that, in their country, children do not invent. They merely adapt. Giant Steps, I am told by the experts, is a variation of old-fashioned May I? One must take so many Giant Steps, or Baby Steps, or Scissors Steps, before one freezes in one's tracks on the way to the goal.

No, not an invention. The continuity remains unbroken. Listen carefully and you can still hear the great dare of "Red Rover, Red Rover, let David (or Nancy or Kevin) come over." Prisoner's Base exists exactly as it did when I was a happy captive fleeing from an imaginary jail. The whip cracks to the same chorus of delighted squeals. But those are not really back-yard games any more. They are played in schoolyards at recess, or under supervision in a gymnasium.

Some things get lost. The finest game of all, the most exciting and mystical and splendid, the game that meant childhood to me, is disappearing—Run, Sheep, Run. Do they still play that in the little towns upstate, in the villages of the West, in the sleepy Southern places? They do not play it in our suburbia. Here, where half the homes come equipped with "jungle-gyms" of expensive steel, where every other child owns a pair of genuine cowboy boots and a cap pistol in an elaborate holster, where an authentic basket is set up on a private tree for a basketball from the best sporting-goods store, children have forgotten Run, Sheep, Run. They are the poorer for that.

We may have played it in broad daylight at times, but I think of it as coming always at the end of a long summer afternoon, after an early supper. For me, the memory is mixed up with twilight and mystery. If you are twenty-five or over and ever lived in a small town, you must have known it. Do you recall it as wistfully as I do?

Do you remember your apprehension as you waited to be chosen for a team? It was a tribute to your popularity to have your name called quickly. Then, when the choosing was over, came the secret huddles of each pack. You had the signals to decide on. Colors they were, usually: blue for "Lie low," purple for "Danger; they're on the trail," yellow for "They're passing; get ready to run." After that came the scattering and the frantic search for hiding places. You went far afield then, sometimes blocks and blocks away. For this was a formal search, with spies and informers and raiding parties; and as it was summer, there didn't have to be an early end to forays.

Do you remember the wonderful hiding places: the nook under a latticed porch, the gully, the cleft tree with con-

veniently drooping branches? And how hard your heart
beat when the enemy (after giving a fair "Here we come"
as warning) started, in full cry, on your trail? Then you
became, indeed, the hunted, the panting quarry. There
was the most delicious danger in the air. You listened to
your own leader, running with the wolves and crying out
words intelligible only to you. You did not dare cough or
move or draw a deep breath. Or the pack passed you, and,
obedient to the signals floating back, you dodged about
in the lengthening dusk, creeping, hunching over, melting
into shadow. And then, after what seemed an eternity of
peril, the shrill explosion of "Run, sheep, *run!*" Your heart
pounded, your legs pumped like pistons. And the light
finally died in the sky, and someone called you in to bed.

The children in our village do not play it. I am not sure
of the reason. It must be because children no longer possess
the streets, as they no longer own the vacant lots and the
gardens. Traffic is too great a hazard, even in our quiet
sector, for such wild excursions. Perhaps there are no
coverts left in which to hide. Or could it be the curse of full
employment among the young? Children belong to the
country clubs, and swim away the afternoons. They go to
camps. They practice tennis and take riding lessons and are
netted into hobby groups. Even those we call the underprivileged go to organized playgrounds, presided over by
adults. One must have leisure for Run, Sheep, Run—leisure and long, lazy summers. Life must not be hurried, as
it is today for everyone. There must be time for the gather-

ing of the clan, time for the chase, and time to come home, shouting, through a dim blue twilight that smells of fresh-cut grass.

Customs change everywhere. It seems to me that summer itself is a different season nowadays, heralded by strange omens. For me it began when I took off the tied shoes of winter and put on sandals for daily wear. It was honey-suckle blossoming on the back porch, and the sprinkling wagon coming down the street to dampen our Western dust. It was choosing up for Run, Sheep, Run. But to today's children only one messenger symbolizes the season. He is their single portent, more significant than butterflies or peonies. He is a man in a white coat who tinkles a little bell and sells ice cream that comes impaled on a stick and in an unimaginable variety of flavors. Summer is the Good Humor man.

# A Garland of Kindness

W E  A R E old-fashioned in our village. I tell you this
in the strictest confidence; we do not admit it to ourselves.
Do our roofs not blossom with television aerials, our
kitchens with mechanical dishwashers? Do we not read
the most recent books, even when we dislike them, and
in our medicine cabinet store the stylish panaceas of the
season? Our addiction to large families and infrequent
divorces we consider merely tokens that we are ahead of,
not behind, the fashion. We discuss the current ideologies,
we speak knowingly of child psychology, we have seen the
newest oddity by Samuel Beckett and the latest show of
Toulouse-Lautrec. Our attitudes are modern, and we share
the modern faults of haste and sentimentality. It is our
virtues that are old-fashioned.

For here we love our neighbor. What is more, we are
reactionary enough not to love him impersonally. We do
not sit impassioned in committee and pass resolutions de-

claring our devotion to him. To us he is not mankind, but man; and our affection warms us both.

Now kindness is a virtue neither modern nor urban. One almost unlearns it in a city. Towns have their own beatitude; they are not unfriendly; they offer a vast and solacing anonymity or an equally vast and solacing gregariousness. But one needs a neighbor on whom to practice compassion. It has taken me many years to emerge from the self-centered cocoon which the city had wound about me, and even now I offer small benefactions with a sort of shyness and am as shy to accept them. So I am constantly being surprised by the matter-of-fact, everyday kindness with which my friends seem overflowing.

Is it the same in other villages? Does this flower blossom in any suburb where the economic soil is neither very rich nor very poor and where one knows the names of at least half the population? I know it does not flourish well in country places, there being withered by the twin blights of spite and curiosity.

Today has been one of the days for counting blessings. Yesterday our village shared with the rest of the Eastern seaboard a storm of spectacular fury. Other communities were treated worse, by newspaper accounts, but we did not escape. We all lost a tree or two (and we are proud of our trees), the shingles of our roofs went flying; worse, the electricity failed and that meant, of course, no light, no heat, no current for the freezer or the laundry or the radio or, in many cases, the important stove. There were evacuations from homes along the shore, there were floods in cellars, lost gardens. But nobody was hurt, nobody minded very much, and nobody I know of went to hotels or Red Cross centers to sit out the debacle. They went to one another's houses, quite as a matter of course. Those of us who had heat took in those without and did not expect gratitude. We helped one another push fallen maples away from walls and hedges. We trekked to the shore to assist in salvaging battered boats. We made enormous quantities of coffee and sandwiches, and we tucked other people's babies away in the nursery with our own. I have just returned from a walk down the street. My neighbor to the left, whose current had returned, was giving lunch to seven children besides her own, all of different ages and degrees of overstimulation. She planned on keeping them for a day or two since at their respective homes there would be no furnaces running for another twenty-four hours. The neighbor to my right was storing in her deep-freeze container the contents of someone else's freezer and inviting everybody to stay for dinner. Farther down three male neighbors were helping a householder patch his roof until the arrival of the uncertain carpenter.

Now all those were kind actions, but not unusual for any community when the excitement of an emergency bubbles in the veins like champagne. What astonishes me in our village is that we continue to be kind when the intoxication passes. We have not acquired the fear of being repulsed, which is the modern snobbery.

We love our neighbor on small occasions as well as large. We visit the sick, we comfort the afflicted, but we are also benevolent toward those whose fortune is as good as ours, or better, so that we win the grace of doing good without condescension. Even the well-to-do are included in our affection. We lend our cars; we admire one another's gardens without malice; we listen with honest delight to the returned traveler in whose journey we could not afford to join; we tend one another's children, run one another's errands, turn taxi-driver or nurse or dog-walker or caterer at our neighbor's signal. We are usually very busy people and therefore capable of accomplishing extra tasks. It is the leisured, I have noticed, who rebel the most at an interruption of routine.

I have nearly forgotten the city ways. Tell me, you people in towns, when your neighbors go shopping of a morning, do they call you first to see if you have an errand that needs doing? If they find a bargain of unusual brilliance, do they fetch it home for you, offering to return the trophy if you have no use for it? When you are ill and maidless, do they send a dinner for the family, complete to chicken and lemon pie? Mine do. The one benefaction they withhold is advice. Our charity encompasses minding our own business.

I know a charming lady who after a number of years of married life here is now separated from her husband. She is still part of the circle as she always was, for we do not believe we must go in pairs, like the animals in the Ark. But we do not know why the separation occurred, and we have never inquired, considering that the *simplest* sort of kindness.

When you go away on a short holiday, what do you do with your children? Hire a strange nursemaid if the ménage does not already include one? We are apt to drop them off casually with friends—there is always room. I know a couple with five descendants all under twelve who went to Key West for three weeks on their first vacation together in years. For this event they *did* engage a supposedly capable woman, paying her a king's ransom. Some days before they were expected back, the woman announced to the family across the street that she wasn't feeling so well and thought she'd have to leave. Did the family across the street—young, with four children of their own packed away in eight rooms—have the kindness to wire the couple at once? Certainly not. They invited the entire tribe of five to stay with them so that the vacation could proceed.

We expect mercies here, not only from ourselves but from others. We make friends with those who are only part-time villagers. We expect the bus-driver to back up for us if we are late at the stop. We expect him to deal justly with the children he takes to and from school and feel we need give him nothing in return except our admiration. Once when my husband was delayed on a rainy night and I could not meet him, the driver carried him to our door, two blocks off the route. And who in the city has for friend and ally the red-haired man who delivers parcels from the great stores in town? *We* have. We meet him in the village drug store, drinking coffee, and he obligingly burrows into the back of his truck for the C.O.D. package we would not have been home to receive. We entrust him with messages for other friends. Once he sat for half an hour with a baby when the baby's mother was called suddenly uptown. If we know him by no other name except "Red," that is not a mark of disrespect. We simply began on a first-name basis.

I find ours a difficult village to live up to. Because I am not so busy as most householders here, I guard my free time more jealously. I shudder, for instance, to think of what it would have cost me to be as generous as another neighbor down the block. She shares with me Jessie, a "cleaning woman" of surpassing talent. Jessie has two daughters, both of whom take piano lessons at public school. They own a childish aptitude but no piano, so my friend permits them to practice an hour a day each on her own instrument. "Tum-tum-tum, ta-ta, diddley-diddlety," it goes every afternoon for two horrendous hours. I, who love Jessie more dearly than a sister, would sooner part with her forever than suffer such an ordeal. Yet I have never heard my friend mention that she considers her generosity more than natural.

Of course, I betray myself when I dwell on such simple instances. The cocoon is still around me, so I peer from it, astonished at what others take for granted. I am astonished at the kindness of policemen stationed at school crossings. I marvel at the patience of firemen rescuing kittens from trees, of the municipal employee who spent half an afternoon explaining the garbage-disposal system to one of my daughters, an officer of her Civics Club. I enjoy the fact that one can never walk to the business section without being offered a lift by every passing driver, stranger or no.

I grow more accustomed, as the years pass, to accepting kindness. But I have never ceased to cherish with affection and with pride an incident that happened soon after we had moved here. I think it was then I began to collect the flowers for my garland, as children collect chestnuts in the fall, valuing them for their number rather than their use.

The war—one of the wars—was in progress then, and the affair revolved about a Japanese family living not far from us. I shall call them the Yamotos. They were pleasant people who spoke English well and were interested in politics only to the extent that they had left Japan because they preferred democratic ways. Mr. Yamoto commuted with the other husbands, and Mrs. Yamoto attended sessions of the P.T.A. and compared notes with the other wives on report cards and pressure cookers. Then an ugly thing occurred. The Yamotos cultivated, like all of us, a vegetable garden where the back lawn used to spread, and one sweet spring night it was broken into and uprooted. Who the vandals were it was never discovered. I think we all prayed that it was children's work. Surely we did not harbor here an adult mind so twisted and vindictive as to consider the outrage a patriotic act! The news shocked me into nausea. Hate, the kind of hate that darkened Europe, seemed to be casting its shadow on our own people. But, true to my city training, shock merely numbed me. I thought of atonement in terms of letters to the papers; my neighbors protested less and did more. By evening the garden had been replanted. There were no public statements, no petitions, no paid protests. Simply, people with gardens of their own came hurrying spontaneously to the rescue with plants, with seedlings, with spades for digging and stakes to drive into the ground. By an act of common love we wiped out our uncommon shame.

Oh, this is no Eden. We have our bores and our braggarts, our snobs and our slanderers. But I believe the scales, if there were scales to measure human nature, would tip heavily in the right direction. Kindness has become a way of life most of us attempt. We do not try to legislate our neighbor. And when we cannot love him, we at least can like him well enough.

I sat three summers before last in a church crowded to the final aisles. It was seven-thirty of a weekday morning, but a third of the village was there. The polio epidemic had struck at a young neighbor of ours and her three-month-old baby; we had come to pray for them. I still recall the emotion of the moment. A few phone calls had been made the night before, a few messages passed. And here we were—the lazy, the beset, the late risers—the men on the way to the 8:02, the women with children still asleep at home. I doubt that we were all stout believers in the power of prayer. But it was the only gift left to offer.

As the world grows colder and darker, we need to remember these things. There must be thousands of villages as old-fashioned as ours, warmed by the hearthfires of compassion. Surely a flame so kindled and so fed can never be altogether extinguished.

# Letter to an Unknown Man

Dear Sir:

All day I have had you on my mind. I woke up thinking about you; and you were there, persistent in my morning thought, while I broke my breakfast egg and drank a first cup of coffee. On the way back from the station (where daily I deliver up my husband to the 8:02) you were so much with me that I very nearly ran through a red light near the village post office. And it was your misty image that kept coming between me and all those household chores which must receive, every morning of my life, a certain rapt attention. You interfered with the grocery list, nagged at me while I watered the African violet, and set me dreaming when I should have been counting shirts and sheets for the laundry.

I do not believe this obsession of mine is rare. There must be millions of women like me at the moment, going about their ordinary human business but doing a good deal of quiet meditation upon you while their hands are busy with other things. We will probably never meet you, never see you in the flesh at all. So far, we are not even certain of your name. But sometime soon you will be chosen to

guide our collective destinies. You are the Presidential
candidate. You are the man for whom next November I
will pull down the little lever behind a curtain not of iron
but of common and rather battered baize.

That November occasion will be cozy rather than dramatic. In our district we vote in an automobile showroom,
and since we are a small district in a fairly small village
there is seldom a crowd. But my husband will be there
behind me, waiting his turn, and so will be a number of
our neighbors. A neighbor will look up our name in the
register, show us where to sign; another neighbor will,
smiling as if this were the government's little joke, check
that name in another book. We will comment on the
weather, inquire about one another's families. And then we
will go back to our radios and our television sets or maybe
merely to our dinner tables, and it won't be your fate
alone, sir, which we will be waiting all night to hear. It
will be very importantly ours. It will be, to a frighteningly
large extent, the world's.

And because my hand must pull the lever soon, is it any
wonder my head is full of you now? You are the candidate.
So you are my concern and the concern of millions of
women like me.

We, equally with our sons and husbands, will elect you
and will bear the consequences of that choice. For I do not
think women go sheeplike to the polls, voting only as the
head of the house directs. Most of us, I suppose, *do* mark
the same ballot as our spouses, but that is more a testament
to domestic felicity than to coercion. In our house, my hus-

band and I have often supported opposing parties and we are rather proud that we can do so without rancor. (We have always felt it was more important to happiness that we agree on the small things like the color of the bedroom wallpaper or whom to invite to dinner than on issues which only conscience can determine.) But whether with our husbands or against them, self-informed and independent or obeying a masculine judgment, we will, most of us, vote. And that is why the thought of you is so haunting now— on this summery day—while you are still a hopeful supposition rather than a fact.

I wish I knew more about you than what I have read and will read in the press and hear at political discussions. Oh, soon enough I shall have a great deal of minor information about you! I'll know your politics, your religion, your height, the color of your hair, your age and practical achievements. I shall probably also learn whether or not you smoke a pipe, what you like for breakfast, and your taste in popular music. But how wise are you, really? How capable of withstanding that pressure from your friends which is so much more insidious than that of your enemies? Do you keep your vanity on a short rein—the vanity which is a greater infirmity to noble minds than ambition? Do you, while we are about it, *have* a noble mind? It is something we need rather badly in these times. But if nobility is too much to ask, is your mind sensible and calm and reasonably clear of prejudice? And when it comes to a fight, are you a good tough determined fighter? How I pray you are! For the struggle is all around us, we are all caught in its currents. There is a terrible need for toughness.

These are only a few of the questions I would like to ask you—questions which ought to be answered before I can feel easy about you. But it occurred to me this morning that you might, perhaps, have your own questions about me. It is possible that I am on your mind as you are on mine. It is I who will help elect you if we are lucky and whom you must serve for the next four embattled years. Sir, I am happy to tell you what I can.

My name you already know, for it is Legion—Mrs. Legion of 12 Walnut Avenue, Spruce Manor. I am one of the Legions whose support you will soon be courting. I have a husband and children and I live in a house on a pleasant street. I belong to the P.T.A. and my children have graduated from the Boy Scouts and the Campfire Girls to junior memberships in our small country club. You can see me in church on Sunday, at the butcher's or the grocer's nearly every morning, and quite frequently at the public library. I read the newspapers. I struggle with bills. I work in the garden and for the Community Chest. I am, sir, an excellent cook. And I try very hard to live within my husband's income and to help him put aside a little money every year—although that is getting harder and harder to do.

And, sir, as much as any committeeman, as much as the men disputing eloquently on the commuting trains, as much as (or more than, it sometimes seems to me) Congressional investigators and delegates and members of political leagues, I am aware of world peril and national responsibility. I told you, I've been brooding a good bit. And since there's no other way for us to talk things over, it might make it easier for you after the convention if I told you now the way I've figured things out.

Not that I think you should listen just to me. That would be putting too much stock in pressure groups, and I'm against them. In a perfectly run democracy—in heaven, for example—nobody would ever have to wire his congressman or send vigorous letters to senators. The best men, the ablest and most honest men in the community, would represent us and we wouldn't presume to direct them when they were debating a measure. We'd let them vote as their patriotism and good sense told them, and we'd be safe. For so often it's only the fanatics, the busybodies who have time to plague their legally appointed delegates with wires and threatening notes. They are the ones who make all the clamor and drown out the rest of us. If you are the candidate I hope you are, you'll listen to your conscience oftener than to a lobby, even if it's a lobby of Legions like me.

But you have a right to know my ideas. And such as they are, you are welcome.

Let's begin, as we must end, with taxes. Taxes are facts —bitter and difficult facts—with which I am well acquainted. They impinge forever upon my life. I cannot buy a quart of gasoline, a package of cigarettes, a purse for my teen-age daughter, a jar of hand cream without encountering them. I pay them when I travel, when I join a club, when I furnish my house or buy a winter coat or turn on an electric light. Whatever I eat has somewhere along the road to my table been taxed. I know about real-estate taxes and taxes on capital gains and the withholding taxes I must pay for my cleaning woman. And I know only too well all about those times in February or March when it becomes clear as winter daylight that we must drive the old car another year or give up camp for the children this summer because of the taxes on our unelastic income.

No one knows better than I, for I am the person who must economize to pay them. My husband has his essential expenses, which are part of earning a living. They cannot be cut. It is I who must ring changes on the meat loaf, shop more carefully for children's shoes and young girls' party dresses. It is I who must, perhaps, learn to give myself a home permanent instead of handing myself soothingly over to the hairdresser. I, or at any rate my sister Legions, have become experts recently in a dozen trades. We paint our own parlors, upholster our chairs. We get along without maids. We can manage an ironer, orange stick, or lawnmower. And we do it pretty much without complaining.

For we believe that we are still the most fortunate women in the world. And we are certainly not so naïve as to think taxes are unnecessary. You are my candidate, and I want you to remember that. Until the great evil which breathes upon this planet is destroyed or contained, we and the rest of the United States must go on spending our tax dollars to prop up less substantial nations or to feed and clothe and heal the troops who defend us. Although I may contend that the tax system has its inequalities and its inefficiencies, not for one moment do I admit we can do without something very like it.

But when my money is being spent I want it spent wisely. I want to know where it is going and why and for what purpose. I want an unpartisan report on Greece and Spain and Italy and on Tito's Yugoslavia and Chiang Kai-shek's Formosa and Castro's Cuba. I want to be sure, too, that every American who gets government aid or a subsidy really needs it. I insist that tariffs and price supports be proven sensible tools and not political instruments. And I demand that such economies as *can* be made *will* be made, at home and abroad.

When our household is faced with a financial emergency—an operation, a new boiler, a roof that must be replaced—we do not hopelessly wring our hands and say, "There is nothing before us but debt!" We pinch a little harder. We trim. We get along without a new car or a summer vacation. It could be done in the national household too. Remember that, sir, and tell it to your cabinet and to Congress. There must be a good many things the government can get along without, to stave off bankruptcy.

And when I talk of being bankrupt I mean it in more than a financial sense. There is such a thing as moral failure also; perhaps that is the more important of the two. This has been no perfect society, ever. We have had our robber barons and our Tweeds. Perhaps we did not invent the spoils system, but we perfected it and made it look respectable. Yet there was a certain lustiness about those transgressions and a readiness to beat them back. They were not like the blight which, somewhere along the line, has seemed to attack our national integrity. So far it has not done more than attack it. It has not destroyed it.

But the disease is evident and must be fought with every antidote in the medicine closet. People, in government and out, have forgotten that we and they are the nation. They have acted, some of them, as if Uncle Sam were a crotchety and crass employer who had to be hoodwinked at any cost. Do you think, sir, that you can make them feel pride again in being a part of a great and continuing experiment? One manufacturer selling on the gray market, one federal employee accepting a mink coat for his wife as a bribe—these are the symptoms of a national malady. By themselves of course they are of little significance. There have always been venal men and, especially, there have been stupid men.

The picture becomes frightening only when those men do not understand that there is anything wrong or unusual in such acts. We cannot hope to lead the world (which we must do even though it is the world who begs for that leadership and not we) unless we are as strong morally as we are in plants for the making of space rockets.

So you must be strong too. And tough, as I said. Oh, but you must be flexible, besides, and not so obstinate that the noise of any opposition will force you to stand by your mistakes!

Are you, sir, able to forgive your own mistakes and correct them? That's the kind of flexibility I hope you have. Or perhaps it's really humility I mean. Humility is cur-

rently an enormous asset and the lack of it has brought
more than one strong man crashing down. There is a sort
of spiritual pride, which some mistake for integrity, that
can be dreadfully perilous, particularly today. It comforts
the bigots and it must comfort the dictators, too, when those
in government have necks too stiff to bend.

So I hope you are a humble man as well as a proud one.
I hope you are a friendly man too, who will like and trust
the people who must elect you. We want to be trusted. We
are used to being leaned on. We women—most of us—will
never be sent to training camps, should conflict come, but
our brothers and sons and husbands will; and (although
less importantly) it is our household dollars which will be
spent. So we would be grateful to be told quite plainly
where we are heading in any crisis. If you are not quite
sure yourself, trust us with that uncertainty too.

We'll happily dispense with televised investigations,
which seem to us the modern equivalent of Roman bread
and circuses, or maybe just circuses. The Kennedy brothers photograph well. It is interesting to watch a labor
racketeer take the Fifth Amendment when he is so much
as asked the name of his brother-in-law's parakeet. And
half a dozen senators in full cry outdo Perry Como for
entertainment. But what we Legions want is *less* entertainment and more information. Are we engaged in a cold war
or are we not? Will it grow into a hot one? Is universal
military training necessary, and if it is, why not make it a
methodical part of our educational system for young men?
This hit-or-miss selection, this "If you don't keep up in

your studies, you'll have to join the Army" sort of threat, saps a boy's ambition. If every youth knew that at eighteen he faced a year's military service, he could make his plans and arrange his future accordingly.

And how are our diplomats doing? What treaties are being made by our ministers? What pacts are being broken? We are not children to be cozened with palatable fibs. Let us have the truth.

To be truthful, flexible, firm, honest, humble, energetic, and tough—that's a long list of virtues to expect from one American running for office. My husband says it's *too* much. But then women are the realists. They are so realistic that they know those are all human virtues, not angelic ones, and therefore not impossible for a candidate to own. And if it is true that Providence always makes a man to fit the times, it is not too much to ask for a hero now.

This summer morning is so beautiful and so bursting with the energy of growth that anything seems possible. So don't be frightened, as you probably are (in a healthy way), at the gigantic difficulties ahead. Don't, sir, let the thunders and the slanders and the great din of a campaign bewilder you. If you are a tough man, we are a tough nation. And the campaign will be over one of these days, and you and I can both breathe easier—for a moment.

Before I say good-by to you (until next November) let me quote something that has always consoled me. Will Rogers mentioned it once. He was talking about the Presidential election, which in his time was perhaps not quite so important to the world but just as clamorous.

"It takes a great country," he said, "to stand a thing like that hitting it every four years."

That's true, and it's useful to remember. Elections have been hitting us, hard, for going on two hundred years; and in spite of everything, we're still a great country. We've survived a lot of candidates. It would be heartening to feel you were one of the great ones that this indestructible Union deserves. Sir, I wish you well.

# You Take the High Road

A GENTLEMAN of my acquaintance suffers from acute euphoria. He is fond of his work, his wife, and his neighbors; he can discuss even politics without a rise in blood pressure; and, except at large cocktail parties, I have never seen him bored. Although he is a slave to no hobby, he is master of dozens, and they are flexible hobbies, adjustable to the climate or the state of his finances. Thus by turns and in their proper season he can fix his attention on gardening, golf, electric wiring, hot jazz, the collection of old glass or music boxes, sailing, or intellectual conversation—and with impartial rapture.

He is, of course, the best of travelers, for he is not put off by the vagaries of trains, inn-keepers, or the elements. And since it is the impact of place upon him and not himself upon the place which concerns him, his expeditions are usually both comfortable and successful.

In a less witty man, this constant good temper might become oppressive. But in him it is a kind of talent, one which translates the humdrum into the enjoyable. All of us, of course, are not so gifted. His talent he was born with as others are born with curly hair or absolute pitch. But even a non-musical child can be taught to carry a tune, and it is within reason that the technique of enjoying oneself can be acquired. For on the simpler levels, is it perhaps anything more than accepting the possible?

Enjoyment doesn't imply gregariousness or high spirits, although the young may think so. A bookworm in bed with a new novel and a good reading lamp is as much prepared for pleasure as a pretty girl at a college dance. Wading for hours up an icy stream, plagued by gnats and uncooperative trout, is not my idea of an entrancing occupation but it's a fisherman's dream of heaven. There are Sunday painters and devotees of the ski, and gentlemen who can lean all night over a chess board. The point is—if they are doing these things for proper reasons—these people are enjoying themselves. They have found an occupation which pleases them.

The trouble comes when one puts on skis or picks up a fishing rod out of duty—because it's supposed to be the thing to do. The younger one is, the greater is the temptation to conform, and it is a temptation deadlier to the female of the species than to the male. So the girl with no athletic ability goes slaloming down a slope, to her terror and her companion's embarrassment. The bride whips the stream behind her fisherman husband and ruins an afternoon and maybe a marriage for them both. The redhead to whom sun is an enemy *will* lie all day on the sand because it is seaside weather. Music-haters go grimly to symphonies in a trance of boredom. The clumsy skate, the timid climb on horses, those with no heads for heights go scaling crags; and all so that some witless beau may commend them as "good sports."

I remember myself in my teens, riding on roller coasters at an amusement park, sick with fright and giddiness, clutching the side of the careening car for what seemed eons of delirious torture, and stumbling from it, when it reached earth again, too weak to stand. I believed that I must pretend to enjoy what my peers enjoyed. But by the time I was twenty and had acquired the courage not to tackle anything wilder than a merry-go-round, I knew a little about what enjoyment meant. It did not include roller coasters. Perhaps enjoying oneself is a grown-up accomplishment, since it implies acceptance. But all life is a process of growing up, anyhow, so the young might as well begin. And there is no better way to begin than on vacation.

Summer is hovering just off-stage at the moment, and soon the land will be loud with tourists and travelers bound to enjoy themselves or die. They will rock on hotel verandas, sunburn themselves into living torches on the beaches, filch the towels at motels, or complain about the service at White Sulphur Springs.

And only a few will find enjoyment. For they will carry their own seeds of discontent along with them, and there is nothing like travel to make those seeds sprout and burgeon. Wives will scold their husbands as intemperately as at home. Husbands will ignore a waterfall to find a golf course no better than the one they knew in Omaha or Westport. Young ladies on cruises (for which they have saved all winter) will sulk in their cabins because so few masculine names star the passenger list. Or, standing on the rim of the Grand Canyon, they will remember only that their showerbaths ran cold that morning. To them new places will seem less important than new mattresses and a well-packed valise more vital than a view.

I know, for I have been myself that sort of journeyer. Travel, like life, had to accommodate itself to me or all was failure. But with the help of years and the euphoric gentleman, I have learned how out of the nettle inconvenience to pluck the flower of pleasure. I will never own his genius for forgetting physical discomfort in the fascination of new places. I still miss a good bed and quietude. But I have learned not to expect perfection. I have learned to weigh the interests of a landscape against a mediocre cuisine and choose which will give me more enjoyment. I have learned how to live for a time with unprivate baths, bores, or inclement weather. If there are no amusing people at the hotel we talk to amusing people on the ferries. Or we just catch up on our sleep.

I've learned two other things: the limit of my stamina, and the kind of travel that appeals to me. So in the mountains I leave the peaks for hardier walkers and enjoy my small strolls in the piny woods. At the seashore I try to establish no new records for either swimming or lying in the sun. And since we both consider driving five hundred miles a day an abomination, we do not go hurtling across the continent on a three-week holiday.

All that, of course, is easier to do when one is no longer immoderately young and eager. I suppose, if it were put up to me, I would trade this ability to find enjoyment everywhere for the zest and the delight and the frustrations of being in my twenties. But enjoyment *is* a talent worth cultivating. The world is wide and very beautiful. It is worth seeing unaffectedly. Let everybody, just by way of vacation, say to himself, "What will give me more pleasure?" instead of "What can I do that the Davises will be doing?" And it's startling how much enjoyment each will discover, even in staying home.

# The Happy Exile

No ONE can describe quite accurately the province of the heart. Ask a man to tell you what his wife is like, and how can he say it? "She has pretty hands. Her hair is brown; one eyebrow grows higher than the other. She's never learned to read a road-map, but she gets up twice at night to tuck the children in." He cannot re-create her image for you because it is at once too familiar and too various.

So how is one to define a region, an environment into which the spirit slips as easily and snugly as the foot into an old house-slipper? The East is my home, although an adoptive one, and it is where I *feel* at home. It has made me welcome since our first encounter. I have known kinder climates, handsomer landscapes, skies more blue and exuberant. It has taken me years to grow used to a mountainless horizon and Aprils that are only intermittently spring. But it is the country of my choice; so I see it too affectionately, perhaps, for good reporting. I cannot even be sure exactly what portion of America the East comprises. When I was a child growing up in Colorado, Back East was

Omaha. Now I go West to Cleveland. Taken as a coherent community, it includes, I should think, only the fairly narrow strip of the nation which lies along the Atlantic seaboard above Virginia. Perhaps only above Maryland. Below that is the South; beyond it is the Middle West, then the West, then the Coast—each with its own look and legend.

But if it is not a large area, it is a most diverse one. New York roars with a voice quite different from the prudent accents of Boston; Pennsylvania's lush farms are immoderately unlike the flinty pastures of New Hampshire. People speak with a broad A in Maine and a small one in New Jersey, nor does Rhode Island have much in common with Massachusetts. The East is a montage. The pictures it calls to the mind are endless and bewildering—the stone fences of New England, New Haven's out-of-town openings, day lilies in June, cities taller and more fabulous than Troy. It is lakes and hills and whaling museums and subways and institutes of higher learning and nearly the world's best restaurants. It is Maine's wilderness and New York's Greenwich Village; prep schools and publishing houses and the Gloucester fishing fleet and factories and gentlemen's dairy farms and Walden Pond; clambakes and brownstones, dogwood and first nights and Ivy League football games; Amish cooking and the aromatic moors of Nantucket. It is old and it is young, conservative and bursting with ardor, very green in summer, very white in winter, gregarious, withdrawn, and at once both sophisticated and provincial. There is no one aspect to its face.

If Easterners have any traits in common, I can think of only two—a respect for tradition and a passion for privacy. Both influence our architecture, our social usages, our way of life. We put up fences; we let our hedges grow high; we cling to houses built in the Colonial or the Georgian or the Federal manner. We are not quick to call acquaintances by their Christian names, nor are we happy about pulling down a tree or a building in the name of progress.

But a love of privacy (a commodity dear because it is difficult) does not imply unfriendliness. We value friendship too much to be spendthrift with it. We simply refuse to force camaraderie on our neighbors with the indiscriminate eagerness of a Newfoundland puppy. One has to get used to a more reticent gesture than one encounters in the South or the West. You may find the Vermont farmer taciturn to the point of silence if it's chat you're looking for. But get stuck in the snow some bitter night and he'll harness a team, pull you out of the drift, and make you a pot of hot coffee without asking to look at your wallet. The Bostonian may live next door to you for years without nodding good morning. But once you meet him properly, you'll know his is the most generous of friendships. Cape Codders are laconic only to tourists. The upstate Yankee is wide awake and comfortable as his opulent valleys. Countrymen in Delaware have a touch of the South in their manner. Pennsylvanians resist change but are easy and hospitable on their native soil.

Environment has been shaping us here for a long time, and it is not a spectacular environment. Our mountains do not tower very high; our chasms do not cut deep. Everything comes on a less picturesque scale than it does beyond our borders. (New York City may make its claim for having the biggest of everything—buildings, prices, scandals, reputations—but New York is not, in itself, the East. It is unique, a New World monument rather than a local town.) We swim in a moderate ocean, drive small cars on less than endless roads. If we like hamburgers rare, we do not care for them raw. Our most persistent symbols are still our quiet elms, our lilac-shaded churchyards, and the fact that brisk marketing still goes on in a shabbily handsome building called Faneuil Hall.

There is something very pleasant about accepting a natural background. I used to wonder why even the most faithful copy of an old house was so much less charming to look at than the original. My eye finally told me the reason. It is because the latter has warped a little with age. All its lines curve a bit to conform with the earth it stands on. Porches sag ever so slightly, foundations swing gently along the ground. Windows lean faintly toward the leaning landscape. The house has stopped doing battle with its surroundings and has become a part of them.

On the literal side, this grace of form explains why many an Easterner would rather spend his money on remodeling a dilapidated farmhouse into a residence than on building a new one at less expense. Figuratively, it accounts for what is most appealing in the East. This is a grown-up place. Here is the undemonstrative warmth of home.

The East is the hearthside of America. Like any home, therefore, it has the defects of its virtues. Because it is a long-lived-in house, it bursts its seams, is inconvenient, needs constant refurbishing. And some of the family resources have been spent. To attain the privacy that grown-up people find so desirable, Easterners live a harder life than people elsewhere. Today it is we and not the frontiersman who must be rugged to survive.

To live in a city we must pay much for little room and have not yet been able to wipe out our slums. To own a country background we must either commute ridiculous distances or make sacrifices of salary and advancement. We have our natural playgrounds, but they are not nearly spacious enough. Our climate is so inconsistent that we cannot even count on the clemency of the out-of-doors when we reach it. We have great universities and the finest of educational systems. But state-supported colleges are few and private secondary schools still outrank their public counterparts. We have population problems and tax problems, traffic jams and tent-caterpillars, high prices and too little sunlight.

What is there in the East, then, that holds us (even transplanted Westerners like me) so contentedly here?

I think the answer is the largeness of this little place. We own a freedom of mind and opportunity not available anywhere else in America. This is not a paradox. We are still rich in one great natural resource—human beings. So diverse is our population, so various its interests that, again like a family, we can have privacy without loneliness. Intellectual or extrovert, tycoon or bohemian, each can merge with his group. Among people of our own fortune and aspiration we can collect stamps, ride cross-country, compose for the oboe, preach on a soapbox, make a hundred million dollars, be an amateur painter or a professional one, play backgammon, cultivate delphiniums, write poetry, or sell all we have and give to the poor. We will not be conspicuous against our skylines.

Moreover, we recognize more than one standard against which to measure success. Mature societies are usually tolerant societies; here there is more than one kind of competition, and a variety of rewards. Mink coats and air-conditioned automobiles and swimming pools and one's name in the paper are all good enough prizes, nor are we above appreciating family connections. But we have other values too. Our rules are flexible. Nowhere else in the country, I believe, is so much appreciation given to merit of mind and personality rather than to material prowess alone.

And for all our moderation, this is the most stimulating region on earth. It is old enough to be wise. It is not too old to have stopped experimenting.

Ungrudgingly, then, we admit to the Californian that he's a lucky fellow in the matter of weather. We tell the man from Alabama that we could certainly do with a few of those magnolias, and we agree with the Coloradan that he possesses some mighty elegant scenery. But we know that scenery is no substitute for conversation and art galleries and windows that open on the world. There are some of us who breathe more easily in a meadow full of daisies than on top of a mountain; and some of us who would rather explore the jungles of Madison Avenue than the Carlsbad Caverns.

A friend of mine who lives in Honolulu is spending a year in the East while her professor husband takes his sabbatical leave from his university. Her family is numerous and they have lived cramped in a city apartment during one of the foulest of our recent winters. I asked her the other day if she was not longing for the return to Hawaii and its spacious amenities.

"Oh, no!" She sighed. "No, no, no. We're all so happy here. I suppose it's ungrateful of me not to miss Hawaii. But somehow I just don't want to go back to Paradise."

No, this is not Paradise or even close to it. But it is home for a certain kind of moderate heart. And while I wouldn't visit here if you gave me the place, it's a wonderful region just to live in.

# The Third Hand

THE mail was late as usual this morning—I think our postman takes a coffee break every half-hour or so at favorite houses along his route. So I was already in the middle of doing my most distasteful chores, answering last week's spate of unsolicited letters, when he came with one more to swell the mounting flood. I have it here in front of me now, nudging aside a half-finished note of mine to a little girl in Kansas City whose fifth-grade teacher has irresponsibly egged her on to Write an Author. I should put it away for another morning's work, but it has set me off my stride —always an easy thing to accomplish. The letter is nothing unusual in itself, being neither so welcome as a fan note, of which I get a modest quantity, nor so dreary as a bill or a request to give my opinion on somebody's handwritten manuscript (no return postage included).

It *is* a request, though. An organization of college women (I shall not name them) desires me to write an article for them. "Out of my specialized experience" is the way they put it. The subject is "How to Combine Marriage with a Career," and they want it not in six easy lessons but in one succinct piece "not to exceed fifteen hundred words." They want to know how I, "as an outstanding example of the Career Woman who is also a successful wife and mother," manage my double life. Not too well, I could explain to them right now, eying my heaped desk, the groceries— since this is Thursday—still on the kitchen table.

My problem is not how I shall answer them but whether or not they will accept what I have to tell them. For the answer is ready. I've had it in my head all these accumulating years. And although flattery will get them nowhere, simple honesty on my part will.

Dear aspiring ladies (I shall write), you have tapped the wrong source. You have called me a career woman, but the label does not suit me. I am a woman, true enough, and I write for publication. All the accouterments are mine—an agent, two publishers, a rickety typewriter, and a flexible contract with one of the major magazines. Those make me an author and a professional; they do not entitle me to claim a career in the strict sense. For at no time has my writing been the center of my life, as it must be, as it *should* be, to the careerist.

What I say may seem disappointing to women everywhere who are ardently searching the horizon for a signal and a beacon. But I think someone should say it. The world is very full of promises for women just now, and some of them are false promises. One cannot pick up a paper, leaf through a periodical, turn the dial of a television set, without hearing the life story of some enterprising lady who is both eating her cake and having it. She is the lady executive with five children and a distinguished husband. She is the movie star surrounded by her little adopted brood. She is the producer, the diplomat, the anthropologist, the fortunate doctor, lawyer, merchant, chieftess. There she is (on the screen, in the magazine photo) briskly smiling while she frosts a cake with one hand and keeps the other steady on some public tiller. What doesn't show in the picture is not only the series of divorces, maybe, the delinquent children, the notebook of the analyst: it's that third hand of hers. For only by having three hands can one possibly juggle those three spheres of wife, mother, and career woman all at once.

An unnatural thing, having three hands even metaphorically, you must admit. Useful, no doubt, but rather a bar to simple, happy social intercourse. Well, so is a career. If one is born (as I was not) to a different destiny from the ordinary, there's nothing to do but accept it. But the extraordinary is never easy. The three-handed woman is going to find life involved, will feel herself always something of a freak and a monster, alienated from simple happiness. And so is the woman who attempts to combine writing or ballet dancing or painting, or running a corporation, with the business of pleasing a husband and guarding a family.

In fact, I'm not sure it can be done at all. One of those fulfillments will have to take precedence over the other.

Lest I sound extravagantly discouraging, let me make clear that when I speak of *careers* I do not refer to *jobs*. There is no doubt at all that a clever and efficient woman —one with the common number of hands—can manage both marriage and a job. All it takes is vitality, brains, luck, superb health, tact, imagination, and a willing heart. But then a job is something which has vacations and sick-leave. It can be left at any time by giving notice, and can even be picked up again later on. It is a way of earning extra money or using up extra time or energy. It is not a whole way of life.

A career, on the contrary, needs the whole woman. It asks all the creative force, the love and pains and fervor, which other women spend on their households. Even for a man the going is not easy if his talent is more than ordinary, and if he carries it to its logical harvest. Even he has to be ruthless and a bit of a monster at home.

For a woman the road is wilder. Wifehood she might be able to graft on to worldly ambition if the husband she was lucky enough to find was a man of great tolerance and self-effacement. But maternity is a career too. Its demands are almost identical, and so mutually exclusive, with those of art. The woman (like the man) whom genius possesses must give up her days, her nights, her ordinary pleasures, the forces of her entire nature. She must be self-sacrificing to the extent that art comes first of all things. And she must be equally willing to sacrifice friends and family if occasion arises. But what we call a "good" mother is unable to put *anything* ahead of the welfare of her children. The state of affairs is probably biological, certainly instinctive; but it exists. Not by accident have really creative women been either childless or unmarried. One can point to the great exception, Madame Curie. One can also admit that

she worked so closely with her husband that their identi-
ties were almost indistinguishable, and add that the sciences
are not the arts. Or one could cite Elizabeth Barrett Browning. But her chief work was done before she married, and
she died while her son was still young. The Brontës,
George Eliot, George Sand, Sappho, Jane Austen—rakes
or childless, all of them. The great saints were career
women of a sort, and a mighty sort. But celibacy was the
norm for almost all. (I am not here including actresses,
although the stage, above nearly anything else, has pointed
up female genius. It is not truly creative enough to prove
my thesis.) I have been taking a mental canvass of contemporary women I know who have been really successful
in both worlds. And if by success one means a single happy
marriage, an adjusted family, a secure place in society, *plus*
the free use of talent and the rewards of that talent, then
I can think of none. I have asked my literary and my painting friends. I have inquired of people in music, and even
business. The answer has been the same. None. The world
has changed a great deal for women, but not that much.
They still have to make the choice between the two goals.

My own is a remarkably unimportant example, but it is
the only one I can speak about with exact knowledge.

To begin with, I married somewhat later than is the
current fashion. I had begun to write for publication while
I was still in college, and by being both single-minded and
single-living, I had, by the time I was in my dwindling
twenties, established a certain small reputation for light
verse. At the time I married I was on the editorial staff of

a monthly magazine, and there seemed a number of fields open to me. But evidently the pull of the career was not very strong. For it was with no struggle at all that I at once resigned from the magazine. It didn't occur to me that there *was* a choice. And for the score and more of years since then I have been a full-time wife with a part-time avocation. Even before daughters put in an appearance, we had moved to this placid middle-class suburb, where the enticements of the literary world would not be too teasing. I have gone on with my writing as other women go on with their petit-point or their raising of prize delphiniums—when and how I could.

Even so, it has not been all champagne or even all beer and skittles. Part-time writing is more difficult than gardening or chairing the local P.T.A. Success, even in so limited a field as mine, brings demand; and demand is a temptation. (Besides, there is always use, in a household, for that extra check in the mail.)

So one takes on an assignment for an article which sounds both remunerative and stimulating to do. One signs a contract for ten poems a year. One promises to finish a book by the end of the winter. But articles have deadlines, and somehow one must meet them and at the same time nurse a child through a bout of pneumonia. Both article and child suffer a little. Or editors must be argued with at the hour the family poodle is producing her first litter. Between the promise of the book and its completion intervene ten thousand domestic hurdles.

As for the poems—how immensely difficult are those

easy-sounding ten! They are not readily composed when help is in short supply and one's mind is half on the dinner and half on the exact and jubilant metaphor. A poet with a poem in mind is like a robin with a worm. Let go the worm (or the idea) for an instant, and both have slithered inevitably away. Then there are the by-products of being a writer to consider—the committees to serve on, the speeches that ought to be given, the personal appearance which should be made. To a careerist they are vital. But the part-time writer gives them up after too many embarrassing cancellations.

I have seen how my male contemporaries work, how their writing hours are guarded, their meals brought into their studies on trays, the house silenced while they create. That sort of Eden I lost along with Eve. Nobody even contemplates guarding my working hours or my privacy. Whatever room I designate as my studio always turns into something else—a guest room, a place for watching television, somewhere to store old hockey sticks and doll houses. And since the present state of affairs is of my own making, I do not complain.

There is only one field where I ever made a real and anguished choice, and that is in the matter of the theater. Tucked away in my head for a long time was the thought that some day I would do a musical comedy. I had the idea for it and a first act sketched out. (Whether I had any talent for it I wasn't sure, but the matter of talent has deterred few playwrights.) I was even bold enough to compose some of the lyrics, once, for a revue which ran a few months on Broadway. But after the Boston try-out, from which I was called back to see two little girls through chicken pox, I decided the musical stage was for those who could remain indefinitely away from home.

I suppose the day is almost here when I shall have time, if not energy, for a genuine career. Or so people tell me. But because I have only two hands it is not yet here, despite one daughter in college and the other nearly ready for it. In addition to the servant problem, there are all the complications of ordinary living which bind a woman so much more than a man to her household round. They are small things: shopping, ordering, planning, taking in the milk and putting out the bottles, answering the letters, buying the Christmas cards, arranging the feasts, consulting the teachers and the dance committees and the dressmakers and the orthodontists. Above all, there is keeping the heart warm and the head clear for adolescent confidences or advice. If I am able to manage these, it is because I refuse to let my allegiance waver; the writing comes forever second.

Does all this sound discouraging? Well, in a way, I mean it to sound so. There is too much glib talk these days about a woman's fulfilling herself. Many a girl feels she is somehow failing her sex if she is content simply to marry and bear a few healthy, responsible children. Perhaps that is not the world's highest destiny, but it is certainly a noble and demanding one, and one no *man* on earth can achieve.

And it will not discourage, in any case, the girl whose talent is so real and strong that it means more to her than any other flowering. She will be ruthless and driven and demanding—as she should be, given her gifts. She will shake off the tyranny of domesticity with an easy shrug. Or, possibly, improbably, she will be the great exception. This is woman's century. She may be the first to attain both the sweets of a good marriage and the absolute harvest of her genius. To her I send my blessings and my awed admiration. But before she reaches greedily for all the gifts there are—before she attempts to juggle two or three lives as jugglers juggle their spinning balls—let her first make sure she has three hands.